It would be hours before help could reach Shane,

Brenna knew. And meanwhile, there was a storm raging. Even if he was alive, how could he possibly survive the night?

"I think I'll have that coffee now," she decided.

Shane liked her coffee. He claimed it was an aphrodisiac and never missed an opportunity to prove it, not since that first time, two months ago....

Two months earlier...

Brenna's fingers traced a path down Shane's heavily muscled arms. He was so extraordinarily male, and the way he made her feel...like she was losing herself and didn't even care.

She told him, "This is a nice couch, but—"

"I have an even nicer bed."

Dear Reader,

By now you've undoubtedly come to realize how special our Intimate Moments Extra titles are, and Maura Seger's *The Perfect Couple* is no exception. The unique narrative structure of this book only highlights the fact that this is indeed a perfect couple—if only they can find their way back together again.

Alicia Scott begins a new miniseries, MAXIMILLIAN'S CHILDREN, with *Maggie's Man,* a genuine page-turner. Beverly Bird's *Compromising Positions* is a twisty story of love and danger. And welcome Carla Cassidy back after a too-long absence, with *Behind Closed Doors,* a book as steamy as its title implies. Margaret Watson offers *The Dark Side of the Moon,* while new author Karen Anders checks in with *Jennifer's Outlaw.*

You won't want to miss a single one. And don't forget to come back next month for more of the best romantic reading around—only from Silhouette Intimate Moments.

Leslie Wainger
Senior Editor and Editorial Coordinator

Please address questions and book requests to:
Silhouette Reader Service
U.S.: 3010 Walden Ave., P.O. Box 1325, Buffalo, NY 14269
Canadian: P.O. Box 609, Fort Erie, Ont. L2A 5X3

MAURA SEGER

THE PERFECT COUPLE

Silhouette® INTIMATE™ MOMENTS®

Published by Silhouette Books

America's Publisher of Contemporary Romance

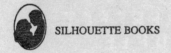

SILHOUETTE BOOKS

ISBN 0-373-07775-0

THE PERFECT COUPLE

Copyright © 1997 by Seger Inc.

This edition published by arrangement with Harlequin Books S.A.

Printed in U.S.A.

Books by Maura Seger

Silhouette Intimate Moments

Silver Zephyr #61
Golden Chimera #96
Comes a Stranger #108
Shadows of the Heart #137
Quest of the Eagle #149
Dark of the Moon #162
Happily Ever After #176
Legacy #194
Sea Gate #209
Day and Night #224
Conflict of Interest #236
Unforgettable #253
Change of Plans #280
Painted Lady #342
Caught in the Act #389
Sir Flynn and Lady Constance #404
Castle of Dreams #464
Man of the Hour #492
Prince Conor #520
Full of Surprises #561
The Surrender of Nora #617
Man Without a Memory #675
The Perfect Couple #775

Silhouette Desire

Cajun Summer #282
Treasure Hunt #295
Princess McGee #723

Silhouette Special Edition

A Gift Beyond Price #135

Silhouette Books

Silhouette Christmas Stories 1986
"Starbright"

MAURA SEGER

and her husband, Michael, met while they were both working for the same company. Married after a whirlwind courtship that might have been taken directly from a romance novel, Maura credits her husband's patient support and good humor for helping her fulfill the lifelong dream of being a writer. Currently writing contemporaries for Silhouette and historicals for Harlequin and mainstream, she finds that writing each book is an adventure filled with fascinating people who never fail to surprise her.

Chapter 1

Saturday

Her pillow was wet. Half waking, Brenna O'Hare turned over. Her cheek brushed the damp percale. She made a soft sound of distress that stripped away the last fog of sleep.

Fully awake now, she lay for a few moments on her side, staring at the empty stretch of bed beside her. The bedspread was still tucked up, the pillows still in place. She'd opened only one side of the bed and crept into it as though trying to cocoon herself.

It hadn't worked. She felt more tired than ever. Her whole body ached, the muscles cramped and tense. But her mind was painfully alert. Fragments of her dreams darted through it. So many dreams, so endless and all the same.

With a sigh, she pushed back the covers and stood up. The floor was cold. In the gray light before dawn, she could see ice along the edges of the windowpanes. That was unusual in late April. Even in Alaska, it was spring. Frosts were certainly possible but this looked like more than that.

Brenna drew aside the curtain and peered out. Her sapphire blue eyes widened. Night had transformed the landscape beyond her small house and everything—absolutely everything—was sheathed in ice. Sunlight danced diamond bright off every tree branch, every blade of grass, her neighbor's truck parked in his driveway across the street, the low stone wall at the far edge of her lawn, everything. The ordinary world had become a wonderland.

Letting the curtain drop, she went into the bathroom and flicked the light switch. When nothing happened, she wasn't surprised. Ice storms like this one commonly brought down power lines. Shivering, she reached for her robe. The furnace would also be out. Time to stoke up the woodstove.

Getting the house warm again and getting a hot cup of tea into herself distracted Brenna for a while. But she couldn't keep her thoughts at bay indefinitely. Work would have helped but she had no classes on Saturday and besides, the roads would be a mess. Maybe later, she could go into the lab, get ahead on some of the research paperwork, but for the moment she was stuck.

She went back upstairs, pulled on jeans, a turtleneck and a sweater, and ran a brush through her shoulder-length brown hair. She couldn't remember the last time her hair had been this long—high school, maybe. She would have had it cut weeks ago but Shane liked it long.

Brenna flinched. She caught a glimpse of herself in the mirror, saw the pain in her eyes, and put the brush down quickly. Asleep, she had no control over her dreams. But she was awake now and she damn well wasn't going to think about him.

There was plenty else she wasn't going to do, either. With the power out, she couldn't use her computer, watch a video or run the vacuum. But she could cook, thanks to the gas stove.

Fine, good that was what she would do. She didn't cook often but when she did she enjoyed it. Besides, there was stuff in the fridge she should use on the chance the power stayed out for a while.

She had the meat browning and was just adding a hefty dose of chili powder when she realized she'd goofed. *Chili.* They'd had chili that first night at Carol and Bob Anderson's. That night two months before when she'd given in to Carol's entreaties and agreed to meet the Mr. Perfect her friend was determined to fix her up with. Shane Dutton. Bob's friend and boss. The guy she absolutely, positively had to meet.

And so she had...

Two months earlier...

"I'm telling you," Carol Anderson said as she stacked petri dishes in the supply cabinet. "If you don't meet this guy, you are going to regret it for the rest of your life."

"I don't see how," Brenna replied. She switched the light off on the microscope she'd been using and slipped the plastic cover back over it. "If I never meet him, I'll never know what I missed, so how could I regret it?" She grinned.

"Because I'll tell you. When he gets married and makes his wife ecstatically happy, I'll make sure you hear about it. When they have their 2.4 beautiful children, you'll know. When they buy that great house in the suburbs, I'll—"

"What do you mean 2.4 kids?" Brenna interrupted. "Does anyone actually think about that? Some poor woman walks around pregnant with .4 kid for the rest of her life?"

"It's an average, for crying out loud, and don't try to change the subject. I am so sure about Shane Dutton being the man for you, I'm willing to break my lifetime rule about never fixing up friends."

Brenna turned all the way around on her stool and looked straight at the other woman. "You? Never fix up? You?"

Carol colored slightly. "Well, okay, there were those one or two times but they didn't actually count—"

"Because they flopped so spectacularly? Let's see, there was Kathy and what's-his-name, Dan? Don? That was, what, three years ago? She swore off men forever."

"She's married now."

"But not to Dan-Don. Then there was Sheila and that guy from Maine. Didn't she say something about entering a nunnery?"

"But she didn't actually."

"What about Barb and that Russian you thought was so terrific?"

"It was a cultural misunderstanding."

"So now it's my turn?" Brenna shook her head. "No, thanks. I'm very happy with just me and my plankton. They don't want to be mothered, they have no gender identification issues and they're not afraid to commit."

"They're fish food," Carol said. "You're having a relationship with fish food. Can I tell you how pathetic that is?"

Brenna sighed. She and Carol had been friends for over ten years, ever since high school. That they'd both ended up in Alaska was one of those weird coincidences life dished out.

Four years before, Carol married Bob Anderson. They were very happy together. Brenna, who had been maid of honor at their wedding, was very happy for them. She just didn't understand why Carol had developed this horrible need to fix up all her friends.

"Have you thought about having a kid?" Brenna asked.

Carol's eyes widened. "A kid? What makes you ask that?"

"I don't know, I just thought maybe if I could refocus your attention away from me and all your single friends, I'd have done humanity a great service. Besides," she added, "you'd make a great mom."

"As opposed to a lousy fixer-upper?"

"You said it, not me."

"Well, I am going to prove you wrong. You and

Shane Dutton are absolutely perfect for each other and—''

Brenna sighed. "Why do I get the feeling you're not giving up on this?"

"Because I'm not. Not for nothing is my middle name Relentless."

"Your middle name is Patricia. My middle name is Relentless. At least that was the joke in high school," Brenna reminded Carol.

"Because you were the only one of us who actually knew what you wanted to do with your life and didn't let anything distract you. To tell you the truth, I wish I'd been that way."

"You've got a good job, a loving husband and friends who think so highly of you they're willing to let you fix them up. What more can you ask?"

"I've got a decent job," Carol corrected. "And don't get me wrong, I'm glad to have it. But you've got a career, something you really care about."

"I gave up a lot to get it," Brenna reminded her gently. In high school and college, and all the way through grad school, she'd barely dated. Except for a brief engagement several years before, her life had been given over to her fascination with marine biology. She didn't regret it for a moment but—

"He's really that great?" she asked.

Carol nodded. "The best, except for Bob, of course, and to tell you the truth—"

"Carol!"

"I'm kidding, honest. I'm crazy about Bob. He's exactly what I wanted but..." She hesitated. "Let's just say Shane Dutton's in a different category."

Brenna's eyes narrowed. "What does that mean?"

"Just what I said. He's different."

"A minute ago he was great."

"Different can be great. You've never been afraid to be different, have you? And that's one of the reasons I think you'll be so good for each other. You're both intelligent, strong-willed risk takers, people who see what they want and go out and get it, and—"

"I wouldn't describe myself as a risk taker."

"You go swimming with sharks for fun. What would you call that, Miss Shrinking Violet?"

"Sharks are very misunderstood. There's actually no danger. Well, minimal danger but—"

Carol held up a hand. "You can tell us all about it at dinner tonight. I'm sure Shane will be fascinated."

"Tonight? Wait a minute, this isn't much notice. I had plans for tonight. I was going to—"

"Wash your hair? Clean out the refrigerator? Clip your cat's nails?"

"You know I don't have a cat, but I do have to—"

"If I'd given you more notice, you'd just have come up with some excuse. Be there are 8:00 p.m." At the lab door, Carol turned back and grinned. "Oh, and wear something sexy. If you don't, you'll hate yourself."

"I will not," Brenna called after her. "Besides, I don't own anything sexy. I—"

Carol was gone and Brenna was left alone to contemplate the gaps in her wardrobe and the craziness of what she'd just done.

* * *

Brenna was still thinking about the craziness when she pulled up in front of Carol and Bob's house. There was a pickup in the driveway. It looked to be a couple of years old and had a few dents in it.

At least that was a good sign. Getting out, she smoothed the skirt of her dress self-consciously, wondered for the hundredth time why she'd worn it, and walked up the path to the front door.

Carol opened the door before she could ring. "He's here. Quick, give me your coat. You look great. Oh, my God, you really do. I thought you said you didn't have—"

"It's nothing. It was in the back of my closet. I don't think I've ever worn it before."

Carol ran her eyes down the very plain, very simple, very unadorned, but absolutely devastating blue silk dress Brenna was more or less wearing. Less would probably have been more accurate. Taking advantage of the fact that Alaska was having a relatively warm and snow free January—as opposed to the lower forty-eight where one blizzard seemed to follow another—Brenna had opted for a dress that otherwise wouldn't have seen the outside of the closet until May. If then. If ever.

Catching a glimpse of herself in the hall mirror, Brenna took a quick step back. What had she been thinking? That leggy brunette poured into a skimpy little dress that left virtually nothing to the imagination wasn't her.

She was jeans and cotton shirts, plaid nightshirts and extra thick socks. She was sane, sensible Brenna O'Hare, marine biologist, shark swimmer, friend to plankton. The woman in the mirror was—false advertising.

"I've got a change of clothes in the Jeep," she said and made a quick pivot on her heel.

"You don't need them."

Funny how she'd never noticed that Carol had quite a grip. It was applied now to Brenna's arm. Short of knocking the woman cold, she wasn't getting loose.

"Bob, Brenna's here."

And that was that. First, Bob poked his head out of the living room, saw her, blinked real hard and grinned. "Uh, hi, Brenna. Nice dress."

He said something else, too. At least his mouth kept moving. Brenna didn't hear him. Because right behind good old Bob came...

Mr. Perfect.

All six feet plus, thick blond hair, shoulders out to here, chiseled features of him. Shane drop-dead-gorgeous Dutton, in the flesh.

"How do you do?" Brenna said.

"Nice to meet you," he said.

Bob and Carol exchanged a meaningful glance and beamed at them both.

They had chili. At least, Brenna remembered that much. She even ate some of it. Bob made very good chili. They talked about work. Bob was a pilot for the airline Shane owned.

"Just a small fleet," Shane said. The man was nothing if not modest. "Freight stuff, mostly, although we do some passenger runs."

"What did you do before this?" Brenna asked.

"I was in the navy," Mr. Perfect said.

"Shane was a chopper pilot," Bob corrected. "He flew in the Gulf War."

Shane looked uncomfortable. "Lots of guys did that."

"He won—"

"Never mind," Shane interrupted. "It was actually pretty boring. A lot of waiting around. Carol tells me you're a marine biologist."

A man who wanted to talk about her work instead of his own? It was true then—if you lived long enough, you could run into anything.

"I study plankton," she said. That ought to stop him dead.

"Zoo or phylo?"

Oh, great. Looks and a brain. Who said life was fair?

"Zoo."

"And she loves sharks," Carol chimed in.

Shane Dutton's perfectly sculpted eyebrows rose slightly. His perfectly shaped mouth lifted at the corners. His perfectly fascinating hazel eyes gleamed with what looked like just the perfectly measured degree of amusement. "Ever swim with them?"

"Have you?" Carol asked him.

"Just once off Barbados. It was a great experience. I—"

"I just knew it," Carol announced and got up to get dessert.

"Knew what?" Shane asked when Bob had muttered something about helping her and disappeared.

"Knew that you'd like the chili. Look, Mr. Dutton, I—"

"Mr. Dutton's my father. He's a nice guy but he isn't here tonight."

Brenna took a breath. This was going to be tougher than she'd thought. "All right, Shane. Look, the fact is Bob and Carol are really good friends of mine. I think the world of them but for some crazy reason, they thought we ought to meet. And I've enjoyed meeting you, don't get me wrong. It's just that now that we've done that, we can go our separate ways and—"

"We could do that."

That absolutely was not disappointment curling through her stomach. "Good. I wouldn't want you to feel as though you had—"

"Or we could get to know each other better." He smiled. "I know I can't compete with zooplankton, but I'm not a bad guy."

She was in trouble. Real, serious trouble. "It's just that I'm rather absorbed in my work."

"So am I," he said, "but I still like to take a break from time to time. Don't you?"

"Oh, sure, sometimes—"

"Good," he said. And that was apparently that.

Saturday

She'd freeze the chili. If the power didn't come back on, there was a wooden storage box on the porch she could use.

Her throat was so tight that it hurt. She brushed a hand across her face and wasn't at all surprised when it came away wet.

Chapter 2

Saturday

Getting to the airport was tough. Four-wheel drive made a difference, and he took it nice and slow, but he was still glad when he finally pulled into the parking spot in front of the low building that housed the offices for Air Aleut. It helped that there'd been hardly any other vehicles on the road. Most people had the good sense to stay home.

Not him, though. He had a payload to fly and fly it he would. A little rock salt on the runways, a little deicing on the wings and there was nothing to it.

Shane grabbed his briefcase out of the passenger seat, slammed the truck door, and walked inside the building. His offices were on the main floor, along with those of several other smaller airlines. In the not quite year since he'd bought Air Aleut, the names over several of the counters had changed, some more than once. There were few businesses tougher these days than running a small airline. If the paper thin profit margins didn't get you, the government regulations would.

But not him. It wasn't so much that he was smarter or tougher than other owners—there were some pretty damn sharp guys in the airline industry. What made the difference in his case was that he wasn't trying to make a go of it with just one small airline. He actually owned half a dozen of them, spread out over different markets across the lower forty-eight. Air Aleut was the newest addition to the company, and therefore receiving his personal attention these days. It was doing well enough that he should be thinking about his next move.

He'd been putting that off because of Brenna, but now—

This wasn't the time to think about it. He had a flight to make. Whatever had been said—and they'd both said too much—it would have to wait. Work came first.

It always had.

Provided *always* meant *up until two months ago.*

Shane stowed his jacket in his office and went out to the fax machine to pick up the latest weather reports. Last night's storm was somewhere over Canada. There was a low pressure disturbance across Siberia that would probably cause trouble in another day or so, but they ought to be in the clear until then.

He got his flight plan filed, then looked at the time.

He had a half hour or so before he'd need to do the preflight check. As usual these days with any spare moments he could squeeze, he knew he ought to get some paperwork done. It was endless and even though he delegated as much as he could, there was still plenty he had to take care of himself.

Resigned he sat down behind his desk in the private office that was a model of austerity. Other executives might enjoy plush work settings but Shane thought that was just plain dumb. It didn't impress anyone worth impressing, and it wasted money that could be better spent elsewhere. On good people, for example. The business was growing but it wouldn't do that on the backs of its employees. They'd get all the help they needed.

They'd get drinkable coffee, too. He grinned as he thought of that. If there was one thing he insisted on—besides total professionalism—it was good coffee. He had too many memories of drinking stuff that tasted as though it had been drained out of a crankcase.

Putting on a pot of coffee, he glanced out the window. Visibility was great. He could see clear across the runways to the low trees in the distance. But the air still had that diamond bright sharpness to it. Trucks were out salting. It wouldn't be too long now before the airport reopened. At this hour, there wasn't much of a backlog of flights. He figured he'd be able to take off on time.

But first the coffee. He poured a cup and was just about to take a sip when the aroma hit him. He'd accidentally used the hazelnut stuff. Why did anyone have to muck up a perfectly good cup of coffee with...

They'd had hazelnut coffee that night at the Andersons. He remembered sitting there at the table, sipping it and looking at Brenna, thinking that he didn't need this, he had enough with the new airline and so on. Thinking how damn good she looked in that little blue silk dress—the same one she admitted later to never having worn before. Thinking, too, how expressive her face was, how easily she laughed, and how maybe it was time to get to know a woman who knew her zoo from her phyloplankton.

Thinking...

Two months earlier...

"Nice dinner," Shane said. They had said their goodbyes to Bob and Carol, and were walking down the driveway. It had gotten colder but was still nothing like Alaska usually was in the winter, or at least the way he figured it was, this being his first winter there.

"They're nice people," Brenna replied. "Carol and I went to high school together."

"So she mentioned. You were the smartest, prettiest and most popular girl in the class."

Brenna grimaced. "She didn't tell you that where I could hear her."

"It was during the standard fix-up speech. You know, the 'why you absolutely have to meet this person' part. C'mon, she didn't do the same thing to you?"

"Well, actually—"

"You go out on many blind dates?"

"No!" She looked startled at her own vehemence. "Sorry, it's just that I actually never do this. What about you?"

"Avoid it like the plague."

They both started to speak at once. "So how come you—?"

Shane shrugged. Moonlight shone on her upturned face. He had a sudden, almost irresistible urge to run a finger along the curve of her cheek.

"Beats me. How about we have dinner Wednesday?"

Her eyes—a remarkably clear shade of blue—widened slightly. "Just the two of us?"

"I don't think Carol and Bob really expect to be full-time chaperons. Oh, and I'm not forgetting what you said about separate ways and all that. I just happen to like to eat dinner on a regular basis and I thought you might like to join me."

"Wednesday?"

"If the zooplankton don't mind."

She was silent for a moment, looking right at him. Slowly, she smiled. "Naah, it'll be okay with them. Well, actually, I think it will be. If there's any problem, I'll just bring along a few."

"They don't eat much."

"Actually, not getting eaten is more the thing with them. Why did you cut in when Bob started saying that you'd won something?"

He leaned against the pickup and studied her. The more he looked at Brenna O'Hare, the better looking she got. Considering where she'd started out, that said plenty.

"You're not exactly into straight-line thinking, are you?"

She shook her head. "Bounce around like crazy. It's one of my many endearing traits."

"It was a medal. Lots of guys got them."

She let that go, sort of. "Did you think about staying in the navy?"

"Sure, but after the Gulf, I decided it was time to move on."

"How come?"

It was a personal question, the most personal she'd asked all evening. She didn't apologize for it. Clearly, if Brenna O'Hare was going out with him, she wanted to know a few things first.

Fair enough.

"I found out I didn't like killing people." He shrugged. "Don't get me wrong, if the stakes were high enough, I'd do it again. But I'd put in my time and there were plenty of other guys coming up behind me. I was ready to go."

"Do you miss it?"

"Sometimes," he admitted. "War's a funny thing. There are long stretches when you think you'll go nuts from the boredom and then suddenly—pow!— you're smack in the middle of it, more alive than you've ever been and just hoping to stay that way."

She nodded and pulled up the collar of her coat. "I've heard that although I'll admit, I can't imagine it."

"This from the woman who swims with sharks?"

"Hey, you've done that yourself. You know it's safe."

"I know, you know, but haven't you ever wondered if the sharks know?"

She laughed. They stood for a moment, looking at each other. Quietly, Shane said, "Dinner?"

He thought she hesitated just the tiniest bit, but in the end it didn't matter. "Dinner."

Brenna lived in a small house on a quiet street in what had to be called a family neighborhood. Driving up, Shane couldn't help but contrast the place with the condo he called home these days. Any place he could catch the required number of hours of sleep and not be bothered by his neighbors was his idea of perfect. Brenna, it seemed, had other ideas.

She had a garden. Well, he figured she did; it was hard to tell this time of year. But walking up to the house, he noticed what looked like carefully tended flower beds covered with mulch, the same way his mother did it back in Virginia. The house itself was two stories, white clapboard with a door and shutters painted a rich, deep blue. It looked friendly and cheerful, not unlike Brenna herself, but with a no-nonsense air he'd be smart to keep in mind.

She opened the door on his ring. He felt a momentary pang of regret that she wasn't wearing the blue silk dress again but let it go. Brenna O'Hare looked very, very nice. She had on soft gray wool slacks, a white blouse with a high lace collar, and a rose wool sweater embroidered with small flowers. Her hair was swept up but a few wisps had wandered loose.

"Hi," she said and stepped back. "Come on in."

"Nice place," he said, looking around. He meant it. The house was tidy, but not too much so. There were books in sight, a fireplace that looked used, comfortable couches and chairs, a few plants, interesting prints on the walls. Through an open door, he caught a glimpse of what looked like a workroom. A computer shared space on a table with a microscope.

"Thanks," Brenna said. "I was lucky to find it. Would you like a drink?"

"A soda, if you don't mind. I'm flying tomorrow. Have you been here long?"

"I came to Alaska five years ago on a research grant." As he followed her into the small kitchen, she said, "It was supposed to last six months but I'm still here."

"You teach, too?"

She nodded. "Grant money doesn't stretch very far. Besides, I like teaching. So, what do you think of Alaska? You've been here what, about a year?"

They were still talking when they got to the restaurant. She was easy to talk with. That surprised him. He thought of himself as being fairly typical of a lot of guys who came up through military aviation—more inclined to action than words. But Brenna asked good questions, and she answered his own with intelligence and humor.

He especially liked that, and sitting there with her, he realized it. Somewhere along the line, he'd hit the age where what a woman looked like wasn't the end-all and be-all. He actually wanted character and brains. Brenna had both. That she also had great legs and everything else was just a plus.

"What's funny?" she asked.

"Just a stray thought," he said and suggested they dance.

He'd picked the restaurant on purpose because it offered dancing, and not the throw-your-back-out variety. Real dancing. Holding her felt very good. She was slender but not skinny, graceful but not limp. Her skin when her cheek brushed his was exquisitely soft. Plus she smelled good.

But then he thought diesel fuel had a nice aroma, so he probably wasn't the best judge of that.

"I'd like to see you again," he said when he brought her back home.

She tilted her head to one side in a gesture he was to come to recognize. "We didn't talk about zooplankton once tonight."

"Disappointed?"

"No," she said and smiled.

Saturday

He dumped the cup of coffee and left the rest in the pot for whoever else made it in. He'd get some of the regular kind when he got back. If it wasn't too late, he'd think about calling Brenna.

They'd both said a lot last night. She'd taken him by surprise, accusing him the way she did, and he hadn't reacted well. But maybe they should talk again, see if they couldn't work things out.

Maybe.

The phone rang, he picked it up, listened for a moment, and nodded.

The airport was reopening. Time to go. He grabbed his jacket and briefcase, switched off the desk lamp, and left. Bob Anderson was coming in just as Shane was leaving. The two men stopped and exchanged a few words.

"You've got the Landers run?" Bob asked.

Shane nodded. "How're the roads?"

"Getting better. Things ought to be back to normal by tonight. When are you due in?"

Shane told him. "There's coffee," he added. "Hazelnut."

Bob groaned. "I get enough of that at home. Hey, how about you and Brenna coming over tomorrow? Catch the game, maybe even cook out. It's warm enough."

Shane hesitated. He liked Bob but he didn't intend to get into the situation with Brenna. That was no one's business except theirs.

"Thanks," he said noncommittally, "but I'll have to get back to you."

Bob nodded. "Have a good flight."

"Sure thing." Shane headed out the door. He didn't hesitate and he didn't look back. Why should he? It was a perfectly routine flight in clear weather in an aircraft he knew well. He'd done the same kind of thing more times than he could count. He had absolutely no reason to think this flight would be any different.

No reason at all.

Chapter 3

Saturday afternoon

The power came back on shortly after noon. Brenna stuck the chili in the freezer, caught a quick shower and headed for work. Normally, she was off on Saturdays, but today she decided to make an exception. She needed something to keep her mind busy. Besides, there was always plenty to do.

In addition to teaching three undergraduate courses at the university, she was also responsible for the research project that had first brought her to Alaska, and had ended up being greatly extended. That she'd come to be head of it at the tender age of twenty-eight might have been taken as proof of her colleagues' trust in her, but Brenna thought of it as just a lucky break. She was in the right place at the right time—when a senior researcher retired—and in the politics of the academic world, she'd somehow managed not to offend anyone, at least not too badly. So now it was her baby and she intended to take it as far as she could.

They were studying the effect of various pollutants on zooplankton, the microscopic creatures that filled up much of the bottom of the food chain. Without them and their cousins, the phyloplankton, life on earth would come to a screeching halt. It would get very nasty, very fast.

The lights were off in the lab, except for the few fluorescent ones keeping watch over various tanks. Brenna was relieved to feel the warmth as soon as she opened the door. The emergency generator must have kicked in and kept the heat going. Plankton were amazingly sturdy little creatures but she didn't like to push her luck too far with them. There were tiny beings swimming in her tanks who represented the twentieth, thirtieth, sometimes even the fiftieth generation of the species she had studied. Crazy though it might sound, she felt a sort of family kinship to them.

"So, how's it going?" she murmured as she bent over to check the dials on one tank. Her experienced eye scanned the turbidity of the water, noting that it looked well within the normal range. Whatever was going on in there, the plankton seemed happy.

She checked more readouts, then took a few samples to look at under the microscope. As usual, she recorded her observations scrupulously. Good record keeping was the backbone of good science. Mr. Dallard, her high school chemistry teacher, had told her that. That was the semester she decided she really didn't want to neck with Bobby Collins in the back seat of the BMW his daddy let him drive. She wanted to study instead.

Remembering that, she smiled. Bobby had been so—surprised? He was captain of the football team, class president, and general all-around stud. The idea of a girl turning him down because she wanted to crack the books would have been laughable, except Brenna meant it.

Science was her way out of the sorrow and regrets, the way of making Da' proud of her, the way to wring a smile from her mom when nothing else could. It became her life.

Until two months ago—

Snapping another slide under the view piece, she restrained a sigh. She really didn't want to think about Shane now. What she'd said…what he'd said…

And yet, she didn't have any regrets. He had deliberately misled her, left her to discover the truth about him for herself. Or at least some of the truth. There were things he'd never lied about, his service in the navy and so on. But it was only afterward, when she thought he was just running small airlines around the country, building a business, that she had discovered there was so much more….

And he'd known how she felt. She'd opened up about that to him as she never had to anyone else. He knew about Da', knew what had happened, knew how it had left her feeling. All of it.

And when she'd finally faced him, told him what

she'd learned, he wouldn't relent on any of it. He acted as though she were in the wrong, as though she had no right. As though their lives really weren't intertwined as she'd thought they were.

No, not thought. Presumed. She'd presumed an awful lot with Shane. In her work, she never presumed anything. Everything had to be shown and shown again. But with him, with what he made her feel, she'd forgotten all she thought she knew.

Two months. Not very long in the overall scheme of a life. Hardly any time at all, really. And yet if it ended now—if it *had* ended last night—she knew that short space of time would always stand out as separate and unique in all her experience.

If only she had known—

Two months ago, if she had known, would she have pulled back? Told Shane Dutton no the same way she'd told Bobby Collins? The thought made her smile. Shane Dutton was no high school boy. He was a man through and through. And more than that, as Carol had said, he was in a completely different category from any man she'd ever known. Devastating good looks aside—and Shane himself blithely ignored his own appearance—he was stronger, more centered, more assured than the vast majority of men.

So why then hadn't he been able to understand when she tried to explain to him how she felt?

Sighing, she turned away from the lab table. There was no point going over and over it. What had happened had happened. Thinking about it just made her hurt all the more.

But it hadn't started out like that. Not at all. In the

beginning had been—what? Laughter. She had laughed more with Shane than she could remember doing with anyone. And she'd discovered how very seductive laughter could be.

Had she been seduced? A faint smile touched her mouth. Well, maybe, but if she had been, she'd been doing the seducing, too. They were both old enough to be cautious. At least at first—

Two months earlier...

"You're seeing him again?" Carol asked. She didn't even try not to sound smug.

"It's just dinner," Brenna hedged.

Carol smiled. They were sharing lunch at the battered old table that took up one corner of the lab. Or at least Carol was having lunch. Brenna was mostly just fiddling with hers.

"It's your third date," Carol corrected. "That's serious."

"Nowadays a third date is serious?"

"Sure. Where have you been? Oh, I forget. Here. Well, lemme tell you, honey, out there in the real world a third date is very, very serious. I know people who have gone years without a third date. People who have forgotten what a third date is even like. People—"

"Okay, I got it. So what do I do? Is this the date where you're supposed to finally be yourself and see if he can stand it, or are you still on your best behavior, or—what?"

Carol put down her fork and looked serious. "It's

a tough call. Your decision, of course, will depend on how dates one and two went. Now I know about one—it was great. As for two—"

"Great, fabulous, terrific, all that."

"Did you sleep with him?"

Brenna groaned. "For God's sake, Carol, who sleeps with somebody on the second date? Maybe I have been out of circulation for a while, but not even I'm that stupid. For that matter, I never was."

"Okay, okay, I just thought I'd ask. So third date— do you want to see him again?"

"I said yes when he suggested dinner again, didn't I?"

"That's not what I mean. After this date, do you want there to be a fourth?"

"I guess…I mean…what are you getting at?"

"If you just want to make sure there's a fourth date, then best behavior again, charming, fascinated with him, etc. You know the drill."

"Boring."

"Very, but safe. If on the other hand, you have more in mind than just a fourth date, if you're going for something longer term, let's say, then this is the time to be yourself."

"Because if he basically just doesn't like me, then there is nothing long-term and I might as well find that out now rather than later."

"Bingo. I always said you were smart."

"What if he isn't playing by the same rules?"

"Whattaya mean?"

"Well, what if he's still on best behavior so I don't get to see the real him and plus he acts as though he likes the real me just to be polite but he doesn't really? Then I think he likes me except I still don't really know him and I'm wrong about him liking me anyway.''

"Then you're out of luck. Hey, I never said this was easy."

"But you did say he was Mr. Perfect so doesn't that sort of imply you thought we'd hit it off?"

Carol shrugged. "I've been wrong before."

"Oh, boy, have you ever."

"Too late. What time is he picking you up?"

"Seven. We're going to the new Mel Gibson movie."

"Then it won't be a total loss, will it?"

Five more minutes with Carol and Brenna would have called the whole thing off. As it was, she went through three changes of clothes—no mean trick with a wardrobe as small as hers—and was just barely ready when Shane rang the bell.

He was wearing jeans and an Irish sweater. His blond hair looked freshly showered and curled slightly at the nape of his neck. He seemed to take up the whole open door and then some. He was very big, very muscled and very, very male.

And he was smiling. Not the phony kind of show-your-teeth smile but the real kind that reached all the way to his hazel eyes.

She took a deep breath and smiled back.

Mel was undoubtedly brilliant. Heck, wasn't he always? But this time around, Brenna couldn't have sworn to it. What was going on up on the screen just couldn't compete with what was happening in her own imagination.

She was vividly aware of Shane seated beside her. The warmth of his body, the crisp male scent of wool and soap, the sense of strength that emanated from him all proved immensely distracting.

And inspiring. Carol's question kept running through her head—and all the questions it, in turn, led to. What would it be like to sleep with Shane Dutton? A slight smile tugged at the corners of her mouth. For sure, it wouldn't involve much sleep. Sex with him would be—

Probably disappointing. A guy who looked the way he did had probably never had to develop much in the sensitivity department. He was probably used to women throwing themselves at him. He probably thought he was entitled and—

Except nothing he'd said or done had suggested he was anything like that at all. On the contrary, he came across as intelligent, considerate and just plain nice.

Mr. Perfect.

Sleep with him? Well, sure, she was thinking about it but it was early yet and she was pretty reticent in that area. Still, it didn't hurt to just wonder a little—

The lights came on. Brenna jumped slightly.

"Something wrong?" Shane asked. He was standing. So was everyone else. The movie was over.

Poor Mel, he'd deserved better. Next time, she'd try to pay attention.

"Fine," Brenna said quickly. She stood and gathered her coat. Shane helped her on with it. His hands, brushing her shoulders, felt warm and hard.

They went to a small Italian restaurant around the corner from the theater. The owner greeted them at the door. He obviously knew Shane. Smiling, he ushered them to a table in a private corner toward the back.

"The usual, Mr. Dutton?"

"Actually, some wine would be nice. Could we see the list?"

"Not flying tomorrow?" Brenna asked when they were seated and the wine list had appeared.

"I'm taking a couple of days off. Did you know there's this thing called a weekend? It's Saturday and Sunday, and apparently there are lots of people who take those days off all the time."

Brenna grinned. "I'll bet I can guess where you heard about this."

"One or two people on staff did mention it. Getting Air Aleut in good shape pretty much required all my attention. But now we're through the shakedown stage. Things are going well."

"Well enough for you to have an actual life?"

He looked straight at her. "I'm giving it some serious thought."

Her throat felt dry. She looked at him over the top of the water glass. "Are you?"

"Seems like it. So, what are you in the mood for?"

"Me...uh—?" A torrid affair? A lifetime commitment? Something in between?

"For dinner?"

"Oh, right, dinner." So much for being herself— or not. She was acting like a total idiot.

"Fish," she said. "Definitely fish."

He nodded. "White wine then. Any preferences?"

And so it went. He was considerate, thoughtful, engaging, humorous, articulate and so on. He seemed to be someone she had known all her life, easy to talk to, fun to listen to, heaven on earth to look at.

And he was serious. Or at least he might be.

She speared a slice of the squid they'd ordered as an appetizer, dipped it in hot sauce, chewed it thoughtfully and asked, "So, how do you think it's going?"

"It?"

"Us, the third date. That."

"Oh, that." He shrugged. "Seems fine to me, what do you think?"

"I'm not sure. Are we still on best behavior or have we gotten past that?"

"I'm definitely not on best behavior."

"Really?"

He nodded. "And I can prove it."

"This doesn't involve dumping the squid on the floor, does it? Because if it does, I just want to get another couple of pieces first."

"No dumping. I've been thinking a lot about sleeping with you. Now if I were still on best behavior, I wouldn't mention that."

Brenna choked. Fortunately, she'd already finished the squid. She reached for her water glass, missed it, hit her wine glass and knocked the contents across the table.

Waiters appeared. They smiled at her apologies,

whisked away the wet cloth, reset the table and had everything back to normal in minutes.

Or as normal as it was going to get.

"You're right," she said. "We're past best behavior."

"Aren't you glad?"

"About that or about the other part?" she asked. "The sleeping part?"

"Hmmm, yes that."

"It's crossed my mind."

There, she'd done it, come right out in the open and told the man she had actually thought about sleeping with him. Her cheeks were warm. Must be the squid.

"And—"

"And what?"

"Do you (a) think it's a great idea, (b) prefer not to say at this time, or (c) would sooner be caught cohabitating with a cousin of this squid?"

"B. Definitely B." She waited, wondering how he was going to take that.

"Better than C."

She laughed. She honestly hadn't meant to. Sex wasn't funny—was it? But she couldn't help it. He was so—okay about this. So completely not making it serious and threatening.

"I think we may be brushing up against A," she said and took a long sip of wine.

Saturday

Brenna put the last slides away, checked the temperature gauges one more time, and sat down at her computer. As usual there were reports to update. She loaded her most recent logs and started typing but the words ran together and made no sense. Several times she glanced at the phone as though that could somehow make it ring. Several more times she had to stop herself from reaching for it.

Chapter 4

Saturday

There was a problem with flying. When it got to be routine, and it was damn well supposed to be that way, it was too easy to lose focus. When all the read-outs said just what they were supposed to say, when there was no turbulence, no weather problems of any kind, nothing except smooth, steady flying, the mind had a tendency to wander.

Airplane designers knew that. They built in all sorts of extra stuff exactly so the pilot's mind didn't have to be engaged much of the time. It was okay to kick back. It was just fine to let your thoughts drift. If anything did happen that you needed to know about, the onboard computer would tell you. Otherwise, there was nothing to do except relax.

Shane didn't want to relax. He liked flying, the real kind, where he got to be a pilot instead of a pseudo-passenger. He especially liked it when it kept him from thinking about things he'd just as soon not deal with right then.

Brenna, for example.

He really didn't want to keep going over what had happened last night. Maybe that was cowardly, maybe it was insensitive, but that was just how he felt. It hurt to think about what had happened and the hurt only got worse when he tried to figure out what to do next.

But the cockpit was dark and quiet. He was alone with just his thoughts. Try though he did, he couldn't deny them.

Two months earlier

"I think we may be brushing up against A," Brenna said and took a long sip of wine.

Shane was just a little surprised by her candor, but not as much as he would have been a week earlier. He'd gotten to know her well enough to realize that Brenna O'Hare said what she thought. In this case it happened to be that she was thinking seriously about their sleeping together.

Which meant he'd better think about it seriously, too.

He liked the idea, of course. She was a beautiful woman but more than that, she was intelligent, sensitive and considerate. What wasn't there to like?

But at thirty-five, he didn't go into relationships

carelessly. His libido might have other ideas—and it was making them clear—but he had a brain, too, and he thought this might be a good time to use it.

They went for a walk after dinner. The streets were full, there were plenty of people out strolling about, taking advantage of the unusual warmth.

"It's minus thirty degrees Fahrenheit in Arkansas," Shane said. "They're closing roads all through Texas because of an ice storm." He looked around, marveling. "And Anchorage, Alaska is getting downright balmy. Think this is global warming?"

"It's something," Brenna agreed. "I can't remember a winter like this. The problem is that with no snow cover, we're going to be looking at a drought when spring comes."

"Then we'd better hope for snow. Care for a nightcap?"

She hesitated the merest fraction. "Your place or mine?"

"As it happens, mine is right around the corner."

"Which explains how the guy at the restaurant knows you?"

"Yep. You wouldn't think it, being that they have tablecloths and all, but they do great takeout."

"You don't have one of those places that doesn't actually have a kitchen, do you?"

"I wouldn't know but if you come over, we could look for it together."

"It'll be a smallish room with appliances in it."

"I thought that was the laundry," he said and grinned.

He had a kitchen. He'd even used it a few times

for something other than making coffee. He also had a fireplace where there happened to be a fire already laid. Shane tossed a match into it and went to make them drinks.

When he returned, Brenna was curled up on the couch staring into the flames. She'd kicked her shoes off and her hair was slightly disheveled from the breeze outside. He thought she was just about the loveliest thing he'd ever seen.

"Chardonnay all right?" he asked.

She nodded and took a glass. "Perfect. This is a nice apartment."

"Thanks. It was the first one I saw when I got here and since it didn't seem to have anything obviously wrong with it, I moved in." He sat down beside her. Warm though it was for an Alaskan winter, the fire felt good.

"Let me guess, you were here a month before you unpacked."

"Six weeks."

"You have yet to meet a single one of your neighbors."

"And they have yet to meet me. We nod when we pass at the mailbox but that's about it."

"It's a little different where I am but not much. Everyone's too busy."

He nodded. "Sometimes it does seem as though we spend an awful lot of time running in place."

Her smile was soft, almost wistful. "That's supposed to be good for your heart."

"I know something better," he said and took the wineglass from her.

She tasted of the Chardonnay and sweetly of herself. Her mouth was warm, soft, pliant. What began tentatively, swiftly became something more.

Shane had underestimated his feelings for this woman. He had flattered himself that he had his baser instincts firmly in control. In fact, he did not and at the first touch of her mouth against his, he realized it.

The knowledge was shocking. He was a man, not a boy. His whole life depended on control—of an airplane, a business, himself. He could not remember the last time sheer, hot, mindless desire seized him so completely.

Dimly, he realized that there was a genuine possibility he had never felt anything like this before.

Which was all very interesting but didn't really help with the moment. Sweet heaven, she felt good in his arms. Her body was slender but strong. She laced her fingers through his hair and kissed him back.

There was a certain tentativeness about the kiss, a hint of uncertainty that he found piercingly endearing. He hadn't asked, and neither had she, about prior experiences, but now he thought he had his answer. Brenna O'Hare might have been around the block a time or two, but she hadn't strayed very far.

Which suited him just fine.

She raised her head, looked at him steadily and asked, "How come a great guy like you isn't married?"

He laughed admiringly. "Flattering but to the point."

"And…"

He settled back on the couch but kept an arm around her. She felt too good to let go of her. "I almost did get married about eight years ago. But she thought I should get out of the navy and into her father's business."

"You did get out of the navy."

"A few years later and then it was to get into my own business. Big difference. What about you?"

"Same here, I almost took the plunge a few years ago. But my Dad was a cop. He was killed in the line of duty. The guy I was seeing was also a cop. The more I thought about it, the more I realized I just couldn't live with the fear that I'd go through the whole thing again."

"And he couldn't leave the job?"

"He was third generation. His grandfather, father, brothers, uncles, cousins...the whole shebang were all cops. The few who weren't were firemen. Besides, he was really good at it, the kind of guy who should be a cop. It was strictly my problem."

"Are you still in love with him?"

She smiled slightly. "Am I carrying a torch? No, I don't think so. If I'd really been in love with him in the first place, I would have found a way to work it out, wouldn't I?"

"Love conquers all?"

"Something like that," she said and turned within the circle of his arm, drawing him to her.

Saturday

Love conquers all. Well, yeah, maybe. But in that case, Shane decided an argument could be made that no one had ever actually been in love. The whole thing was a sham, a fantasy concocted by poets, singers, gift card companies and certain novelists. Lust existed, that was certainly real. And unlike plenty of guys he knew, Shane actually believed friendship was possible between men and women. He couldn't say he'd ever experienced it but he thought he'd come pretty close with Brenna.

Until…

He shook his head, angry at the direction of his thoughts, and glanced at the controls. Situation normal. Totally, boringly normal. But that was good, he reminded himself. Uneventful was exactly what every flight was supposed to be.

He sighed and glanced out the window. At eighteen thousand feet, he normally would have had a great view but clouds appeared to be moving in. Shane frowned. It probably didn't mean anything but he'd expected completely clear weather. That front over Siberia must be moving faster than predicted.

He checked his watch. He was just about two hours from his destination, a small town in northern Alaska. Figure an hour or so on the ground—people up there generally liked to chat with the pilots who dropped in and Shane didn't begrudge them—then home. He still ought to beat the weather.

But he couldn't beat his thoughts. Like it or not, they kept returning to Brenna.

Two months before…

Brenna used a lilac-scented soap. At least, he thought it was lilac. It reminded him of warm summer nights, waking to the same scent wafting through open windows, drowsing half dreaming, content.

But Shane was far from content now. On the contrary, the driving hunger that seized him was sudden, raw and all but irresistible. This was no slow gathering of desire, no leisurely awakening of the body. This was hard, immediate and demanding.

He drew a ragged breath, distantly aware that his heart was pounding, and tore his mouth from hers. Her eyes were very wide and slightly dazed. Good. He'd hate to think he was the only one going through this.

His lips grazed her throat. She moaned and twined her arms around him. Together, they slipped down onto the couch. Her body was soft and pliant beneath his. He slipped a hand under her skirt, lifting it slowly and encountered—

A low chuckle broke from him. She was wearing stockings and a garter belt, not panty hose. "An old-fashioned girl," he murmured and stroked his palm along her thigh.

Her hips arched against him. "Worse, a lingerie addict."

He sat up slightly. She looked flushed, her lips were full, ripe, tantalizing. "Really?"

"It's my secret vice."

"Lucky me," he murmured and cupped her buttocks in his hands, squeezing lightly.

She ran her hands over his sweater and smiled. "Aren't you getting awfully hot?"

"Tremendously." He pulled the sweater over his head and tossed it onto the floor. Removing it didn't seem to help at all. Flames licked up and down his spine.

Brenna touched his chest tentatively. Her fingers circled a button.

"They come undone," he said.

They did. He helped her pull the shirt out from his belt. When she finished with the last button, she separated the two halves slowly and laid her hands flat on his chest. Her touch felt like cool silk. His self-control teetered one step closer to the edge.

Her gaze was frankly admiring as she eased the shirt from the broad expanse of shoulders. "I thought pilots just sort of sat there," she said.

"I row." His voice was husky. He hadn't felt like this since—since when? His memory seemed to be going. But then more than a little of his brain appeared to be shutting down.

"Row?"

"On a machine, in a boat, anywhere I can. It's great exercise."

"Apparently." Her fingers traced a path down each of his heavily muscled arms. "Did you ever wonder why nature made males stronger than females?"

"Just for the fun of it?"

Her smile was long, slow and delicious. "Could be." She shifted slightly under him. "This is a nice couch but—"

"I have an even nicer bed."

"Do you really?"

"You could decide for yourself."

One of her delicately arched eyebrows rose ever so slightly. "I think I already have."

Chapter 5

Saturday

A gust of cold air hit Brenna as she stepped outside the laboratory building. Instinctively, she drew her jacket more tightly around herself. In the few hours she'd been inside, the temperature had fallen sharply. Shivering, she hurried for her car.

It took a few minutes of sitting in it with the engine going and the heat turned up before the shivering stopped. She noticed several other people dashing across the parking lot, as ill-dressed for the sudden change in weather as she was herself.

"Winter's back," she murmured as she shifted into Drive. Not only that, but clouds were moving in fast. It actually looked as though there might be snow. She flipped the radio on in time to hear a weather report.

"...fast-moving Siberian low getting ready to sock us, folks. Give the furnace a little extra pat and check the battery supply. Hate to say it but we could be looking at more ice than snow. Stay tuned for..."

"Great," Brenna muttered. She switched the radio off, signaled and switched lanes. She'd better stop at the market.

Most of Anchorage seemed to have the same idea. She did manage to get a parking spot but just barely. There were no carts left but she snagged a basket. In the six years she'd been in Alaska, she'd become accustomed to people taking the weather in stride. The local TV stations loved to run stories about folks in the lower forty-eight panicking because a few inches of snow were on the way. But this was different. Even hardened Alaskans knew to take ice seriously.

Fighting the impulse to buy things she would never have bothered with normally—plum sauce, kiwis, tomato pasta—she got the basics and got in line. Half an hour later, she was back in the car, counting herself lucky. As she pulled out of her spot, horns went off. Four drivers tried to shimmy in right behind her. One made it. The others honked, gestured and rolled down their windows.

Traffic was heavier than usual, all those people out shopping, but she got home without any problem. Usually she left her car outside but tonight the garage seemed like a good idea. She'd never bothered with an automatic door so that meant getting out, opening the door, and then figuring out what she needed to move to make room for the car. Fortunately, it wasn't much. The car and Brenna herself were snug inside just as the first flakes came down.

At least they were flakes. Glancing out the living room window, she thought maybe the forecast would be wrong. They'd just get some much needed snow and that would be that. By morning, everything would be back to normal.

Or it wouldn't. Even as she stood there watching, she heard a ping against the pane of glass, followed by another and another. Within minutes, the soft, downy fall of snow had turned into the hard assault of sleet.

With a sigh, she turned away and went to stoke the woodstove. The furnace was working fine, with or without a pat, but the woodstove made the soul warmer. That done, she glanced around. She'd cooked that morning. There wasn't a whole lot left to do.

"I could vacuum," she murmured and reflected, not for the first time, that she was showing a tendency to talk to herself. It must be the effect of living alone for a sizable chunk of her life.

Seven years she'd been on her own, six of them here in Alaska. That was almost one quarter of all her years on the planet. Time was passing. Before she knew it, she'd be in her thirties, then her forties, and then—

"Oh, for heaven's sake." Exasperated with herself, she glanced around again for something to do. The small house was too tidy. She was a habitual picker-upper, the sort of person who just automatically put things away where they belonged. She knew that was part of her scientific training but there were still times when she regretted it. Short of dragging out the vacuum or scrubbing the bathtub, she might as well twiddle her thumbs.

Or read. She'd curl up with a good book, one of the several she hadn't had a chance to get to in the past two months. She'd read the rest of the day away, read far into the night, fall asleep with her light still on and never think about Shane, what he was doing, whether he was going to call. Never think of him at all.

Right.

She made tea, nice, soothing herbal tea. She put on a CD, nice, soothing Bach. She picked up a book, nice, soothing… She dropped the book. It had one of "those" covers. The last thing she needed was something torrid. Maybe a mystery—

Brenna settled down on the couch, opened the book, started to read. The pillow needed adjusting. The light wasn't quite right. She felt a little chilly, maybe she needed a blanket. She got a blanket, sat down again, put the blanket over her knees, picked up the book—

The blanket was itchy. She took it off, refolded it, put it back in the linen closet and got back to find her tea was getting cold. She made new tea. Bach finished. She put on her favorite Clannad album, sat down on the couch again, picked up the book—

The woodstove could probably use another couple of pieces of wood. She put them in, sat down again, picked up the book—

Was that a faucet dripping? She got up, checked the kitchen sink, checked the downstairs bathroom, decided it was the sleet outside that was getting heavier, turned the thermostat up slightly and sat down. Again.

Clannad finished. Brenna remembered thinking about getting a multi-CD changer a few months before, regretted not doing it, got up, put on Copland's *Appalachian Spring*—maybe it would drown out the sleet—and sat down. Again.

She opened the book, started reading, realized she'd read it before, and got up to get another book. Her hand fell on a biography of Franklin and Eleanor Roosevelt she'd been dying to read. She snatched her hand away. Shane had given her the book.

She grabbed the first book she happened to touch. It was an anthology of romantic poetry she'd had since college days. She and Shane had read parts of it to each other one rainy afternoon when they—

Fine, forget books. She'd read magazines. She had several pounds of scientific journals just begging for her attention. She'd plow her way through every last one of them.

Her tea was cold again. She poured it down the sink and made hot chocolate instead—with extra marshmallows. Shane didn't like marshmallows, unless they were toasted over a campfire as he and his brothers had done every summer when he was growing up. He'd told her about that during long talks they'd had walking hand in hand, or nestled together in bed, or over the breakfast table—

She really didn't want the hot chocolate. She didn't want to read the journals, either. She'd take a nice, long bubble bath instead. One of the best features of her house was the big old Victorian style bathtub upstairs. Shane especially liked it because it was big enough for two—

She didn't need a bath. She'd…iron. Yes, that was it. She'd find something totally mindless to watch on TV and iron. Briskly, Brenna got out the board, found the basket of clothes that needed pressing, got everything set up, adjusted the iron to the right temperature and was just about to flick on the TV when the phone rang.

Brenna jumped. Her feet didn't quite leave the floor but they came close. Her heart slammed against her ribs.

This was ridiculous. Absolutely, totally ridiculous. She ought to have more control over herself. She was too old to be so absurdly vulnerable. Just to prove it, she'd let the answering machine take the call.

The machine was programmed to pick up on the fourth ring. Brenna lasted through three. She grabbed the receiver, took a deep breath, and said, "Hello."

"Hi, it's Carol."

Brenna sagged. She told herself she hadn't expected it to be Shane and didn't even necessarily want it to be. But the words rang hollow.

"Hi," she said, so cheerfully that she came close to sounding perky.

Silence. Slowly, Carol said, "Everything okay?"

"Sure, fine, of course. Some weather though. Everything all right with you guys?"

"Sure, I guess. Bob's at work so I'm just sort of hanging out. I heard a few places have lost power. You?"

"It was off for a while this morning, but it's back on now. Is this supposed to last much longer?"

"Through the night at least and it could be more. Anyway, I was wondering if it's not too bad tomorrow, would you and Shane like to come over for dinner?"

"I...uh..."

"You could ask him when he gets back from his flight."

"He's flying today?"

"He's got a run up north. He didn't mention it?"

"I must have forgotten. I'll have to get back to you about dinner."

"No problem. You're okay though?"

"Of course. Look, I'd better go..."

"Let me know if you can come."

Brenna assured Carol that she would and hung up. She liked Carol enormously but she felt utterly unable to confide in her about Shane. It just hurt too much.

So he was flying. Why not? That was what he did. At least it was just a routine run. There was no reason to think the weather would cause him any problems. No reason at all.

Chapter 6

Saturday

Shane cursed softly under his breath. Two minutes ago, not more, the feel of the plane had changed. It wasn't all that much and plenty of people would never have noticed it. But his senses were so well attuned to the machine that he had felt the change immediately. There was a certain heaviness, a hesitation that hadn't been there before.

He was icing up. A glance out the cockpit windows confirmed it. A thin coating of ice was forming on both his wings. He straightened, took a firmer hold on the controls and went through a split-second checklist of what to do. If he stayed at this altitude, ice would continue to form. Standard procedure called for a descent of several thousand feet into warmer air.

He was outside Anchorage airspace, so there was no need to check in with the controllers. He tipped the nose down gently and kept an eye on the altitude gauge. At thirteen thousand feet, he leveled off. That should do it.

The cloud cover was heavy but he was steady on course, about an hour from landing. He started to settle back again. A small tremor went through the plane, so slight he thought for a moment that he'd imagined it. He hadn't.

Shane looked out the window. With the clouds so thick, it was hard to see but it seemed as though the ice on the wings, far from lessening, was building even more quickly. The entire plane shuddered. As with all aircraft, there were tolerance limits on how much weight the plane could bear, especially on the slender wings. He was approaching those limits rapidly.

He edged the nose down again and continued his descent. At nine thousand feet, he leveled off and waited. He had gotten to the point where terrain could become an issue. Thinking that, he grimaced. It was pilot talk for mountains. You really didn't want to pop out of a cloud all of a sudden and find yourself about to fly into space already occupied by a mountain. The mountain always won.

On the other hand, he couldn't climb because ice would just keep accumulating and he'd lose control of the craft before much longer. There was no choice but to hold steady and hope for the best. Keeping one hand on the wheel, he fished out his terrain maps and took a quick glance. It looked as though he ought to be okay. If nothing else went wrong.

He waited, counting off the minutes. At this altitude, there should be warmer air to melt the ice off the wings and restore the plane to its normal feel. It shouldn't take long.

The plane shuddered again. He cursed and tried to see out the window. The ice definitely wasn't melting. It still appeared to be getting worse. The explanation sent a lightning-bright flare through his brain. The Siberian front must have moved in so fast that it wedged under the existing front, creating a temperature inversion. Seeking warmer air, he'd flown into colder.

And now he had a real problem.

He also had very little time left to find a solution to it.

Brenna popped a couple of slices of bread in the toaster, pushed the lever down and waited. She wasn't really hungry but toast was good comfort food and she felt in the mood for that. Ever since she'd gotten off the phone with Carol, she felt vaguely uneasy. It was difficult to explain, if not impossible, but a sense of apprehension was growing inside her. She tried to shake it off but it kept returning. Like it or not, she had the overpowering feeling that something was wrong.

Well, of course it was. She and Shane had argued last night. Their relationship was strained, at the very least, and might even be over. How was she supposed to feel—great?

The toast popped up. She spread softened butter on it and took a bite, still standing at the window. Sleet continued to pelt against the glass. The lights had flickered twice but so far power was holding. Still, it would probably be a good idea to get the oil lamps out and make sure they were ready to go. She'd do that as soon as she finished the toast. Then maybe she'd fill the bathtub with water. If very many lines went down, it could be a day or two before they were fixed. Better to be prepared.

She picked up the last few crumbs with the pad of her finger, licked them off and put the plate in the dishwasher. The oil lamps were on the lower shelf of her storage closet. She got them out, poured in fuel, and secured the lids again. Leaving them on the kitchen counter, she went upstairs.

On second thought, filling the bathtub seemed silly. She had the standard supply of bottled water and that should be enough. A hot shower was a lot more appealing. She turned the taps on, pulled the curtain closed, and got undressed. The mirror in the bathroom steamed up quickly. She stepped under the water and let it flow over her. Some of her tension eased but she still felt that odd prickling at the back of her neck that she couldn't seem to shake.

Shane checked the altitude gauge and heading, and reached for the radio. "Anchorage Tower, Anchorage Tower, this is Aleut niner-four-niner. Come in."

Nothing. Great. They'd be busy in the tower. He wouldn't have top priority. But he could get it and fast. All he had to do was announce that he was declaring an emergency. Of course, the second he did that he condemned himself to a full-fledged inquiry and approximately three tons of paperwork.

And he could still hit warmer air any minute.

It was a judgment call. He'd made thousands of them over the years, when he was a kid learning to fly out of the local airfield, in the navy and ever since. He made them calmly and rationally. If you did it any other way, you usually didn't get a chance to do it again.

He edged the nose down. If he was dead on course and if the maps were right, he could risk another few thousand feet. If.

The engines had started to whine. He'd better find that warmer air fast or there was only one way this was going to end.

The altitude gauge ticked off the numbers—down one thousand, one-three, one-five, one-eight. The whining got louder. The plane was jerking worse than a bronco.

Time to take a straight-on look at reality. He flicked the radio again. "Anchorage Tower, Anchorage Tower, come in. This is Aleut niner-four-niner, declaring an emergency. Repeat, Aleut niner-four-niner, declaring an emergency."

Instantly, a voice came back. "Aleut, niner-four-niner, this is Anchorage Tower. What's the problem?"

"Ice on the wings building fast. I'm down to six thousand feet and falling. Heading..." He rattled off the numbers, watching the gauges all the while. Back in the navy, he'd had a nice ejection seat and a parachute. A guy could get nostalgic for that kind of thing.

"Roger, Aleut niner-four-niner, we comp. Nearest airfield is forty-five minutes on your course."

The entire plane spasmed. Shane had never felt anything like it in his life but he knew what it was anyway. As they liked to say on "Star Trek," hull integrity was being breached. Translation: his aircraft was being ripped apart.

"Roger, Anchorage Tower, doesn't look like an option. I'm coming down now."

"Understood, Aleut niner-four-niner." Behind the calm voice of the controller, speaking more rapidly now, Shane could just catch the murmur of other voices. The moment he declared an emergency, everyone in the tower knew it. They'd all be watching—and hoping.

"Confirm course heading, Aleut niner-four-niner," a new voice said. That would be the senior controller on duty. He'd be starting the procedure already for locating a downed plane. Shane had seen it done dozens of times, had participated in it himself more than a few times. He'd just never needed to be on the receiving end before.

Shane rattled off the numbers again. He had to pray they were right. With the battering the plane was taking, there was no guarantee that the instruments were accurate.

Not that he could afford to worry about that right now. He was over rugged terrain. The chances of finding somewhere to put down were just about nil. At the absolute best, he was looking at a crash landing.

He checked his belts and strained to see through the windshield. If the clouds would just clear enough for him to get a glimpse of what lay below—

As though in answer to his wish, he broke through suddenly into open air. One look down was enough to tell him just how bad the odds really were. The good news was that there were no mountains in sight. The bad news was that there was no flat ground, either. Somewhere way back in time earthquakes must have rippled across this part of Alaska. The ground looked as though waves had become permanently fixed in it. A crash landing wasn't in the cards. It was going to be just a plain old crash.

"Anchorage Tower, Aleut niner-four-niner, going down." Even as he spoke the words, he knew they might very well be his last.

A burst of static came back. "...Aleut...niner... comp...air rescue...good..."

The plane spasmed again. A high, shrill ripping sound filled the cockpit. The ground rushed up to meet him.

Brenna got out of the shower and reached for a towel. She wrapped it around herself, took another and began towel drying her hair. She'd probably used up her entire supply of hot water but she did feel better. She finished with her hair and used the towel to wipe the condensation off the mirror. A glance in it surprised her. Her eyes seemed wide and dark, and her face looked very pale. Must be a trick of the light. She felt fine, just that odd prickling sensation that seemed bound and determined not to go away.

Plugging in the blow dryer, she bent over slightly and let the hot stream of air pour over her hair. It took a long time to dry fully. When she was done, the air in the bathroom had begun to cool. She put on a robe and went downstairs to see if she could catch a weather report.

The phone was ringing.

Chapter 7

"Brenna?"

It was Bob's voice. The first thing she thought was that he didn't know Carol had already called. Hard on that came the realization that he sounded—odd, somehow.

"Hi, Bob. How are you?"

"Okay, listen..."

"About dinner tomorrow, I talked with Carol awhile ago."

"I know...look..."

"I appreciate the invitation. I just don't know if—"

"Brenna, honey, it's not about dinner."

Bob had never called her honey. He just wasn't the kind of guy who did that. And there definitely was something wrong with his voice.

Something wrong.

She sat down on the couch, her hand suddenly tight around the phone. "What is it?"

He was silent for a moment. She could hear him take a deep breath. There was noise in the background, voices. It sounded as though he were calling from somewhere very busy.

"Shane's down, honey. I wish to God there was some better way to say it but that's just how it is. The good part is that he was in touch with the tower and they got his heading. As soon as the weather clears even a little—"

"Down?" Down where? Down in the lower forty-eight? Down south? Down under?

"Carol's gonna come over there, okay? She's leaving now. It won't take her long. Look, you've got to know everybody's going to be doing everything possible. Absolutely everything. And Shane, hell, he's the best pilot I've ever seen. Nobody handles a plane better than him."

"He crashed…?" She heard her own words as though from a very great distance. The wall opposite where she was sitting seemed to be flying away from her at an enormous speed.

She couldn't breathe.

"We don't know that. There's a chance he had some control left during the descent."

"He didn't crash…?"

"I don't know, honey. I wish I did. The tower lost radio contact with him there at the end and—"

"Oh, God."

"But that doesn't mean… Look, Carol's on her way. When she gets there, you tell her to call me, okay? Maybe we'll know something more by then. Okay?''

"Yes, all right, I'll tell her—" Brenna hung up but didn't move. If she did, she would shatter. She put her arms around herself and pressed hard, as though trying to hold all the little pieces together.

It hurt so much. She rocked forward, moaning. Images from the past darted through her mind—her mother, eyes haunted, anguished; her aunts and uncles gathering in small, hushed knots, their faces strained; the men in uniform who came and went, quietly murmuring, their glances filled with pity when they fell on her.

It was all happening again. Finally, after so long, she had dared to really let herself feel for someone, even to love, and now this. This horrible, agonizing, hideously familiar thing called death.

Shane couldn't die. No, he absolutely couldn't. He wasn't dead. She must not even think it was possible. Fiercely, Brenna scrubbed at her cheeks, denying the tears that had begun to slip silently down one by one. Shane was alive. He had to be.

But if he wasn't…or if he was alive but hurting, dying, alone… A sob broke from her. She rocked forward again, trying so hard to hold herself together.

"Just go. Leave me alone."

The last words she had said to him echoed through her mind. She bit her lower lip so sharply that droplets of blood appeared. It was the weather, the ice. Bob had said. It wasn't her fault. She hadn't done this any more than she had with her father….

"Go away. I don't want to listen to you any more."

She'd been fourteen years old and desperate to escape her parents' rule, longing to be done with growing up.

"Go away."

And he had, forever, dead in an alley scant hours later after that final, stupid fight.

And now Shane...

It wasn't her fault. In fact, it wasn't about her at all. The only person who mattered here was Shane. She had to get control of herself. He was a proud, good man and he had cared for her. She knew how he would expect her to behave.

She got up and went upstairs. Climbing the steps one tread at a time, she suddenly felt terribly old.

In her bedroom, she put on jeans and a sweater, brushed her hair and clipped it back in a ponytail. Her eyes stood out more starkly than ever, the only color in her face.

A car pulled into the driveway. Brenna hurried downstairs and had the door opened as Carol came up the walk. They embraced.

"I'm so sorry," Carol said softly. "So very sorry."

Brenna nodded. It was so very hard not to cry but she was determined. "So am I. But Bob said, he's a great pilot."

"The best and they know where he was when...when it happened. They know exactly where to look. As soon as the weather clears at all—"

"I know," Brenna said. Unspoken was the thought that the rescue workers rarely found anyone alive in such circumstances. They mainly recovered bodies.

But she wasn't going to think that and she certainly wasn't going to say it.

"I really appreciate your coming over," she said, "but if I'd been thinking more clearly, I would have told Bob that you shouldn't. The roads must be terrible."

"It was a little exciting," Carol admitted. "But there's no way I wouldn't have come. This is a tough time but you're going to get through it okay. So's Shane."

Brenna nodded, not trusting herself to speak. After a moment, she said, "Bob wanted you to call him."

"Fine, then what do you say we get out a deck of cards and see if you're still such a hotshot gin rummy player?"

Bob had no new news. He just said again that everything that could be done would be done, and promised to keep in close touch.

Carol shuffled the cards. They played a hand, then another. Time passed. Brenna had no real idea how much. Part of her thought hours had gone by, but another part thought that everything was all part of the same endless moment, the one that had started when she learned about Shane.

Finally, Carol put down her cards. "You owe me 1,346 toothpicks. The most I ever won from you before was forty."

"I guess I'm not such a hotshot anymore. So, what're you going to do with them?"

"We're putting an addition on the house. Sure some people would say building it out of toothpicks is doing it the tough way, but we say why should

wood be any different just because it comes in teeny,
tiny pieces?''

''Why indeed?''

Carol looked at her. ''You know it's okay to cry.''

''If I start, I'm not sure I'll stop, so I think it's
better if I don't start.''

''Whatever you say. I'm going to fix us something
to eat. You have a preference?''

''I'm not hungry but you go ahead. I made chili
this morning.'' Was it only this morning? It seemed
like another lifetime. ''It's in the freezer.''

''Please don't take this the wrong way, but chili's
not my big favorite.''

''But you eat Bob's chili all the time.''

''Exactly. That's the sum total of my chili-eating
needs. Truth be told, it's far beyond them but he's so
proud of that stuff I can't say no.''

Brenna nodded. Her eyes felt very hot, burning
even. ''It's funny, isn't it? People go on and on about
love like it's some huge, mysterious thing. But it isn't.
It's all right there in the small, everyday parts of life,
like eating the guy's chili.''

Carol put a hand gently over hers. ''He drinks my
coffee.''

''You make great coffee.''

''How about I make some to go with a couple of
grilled cheese sandwiches? If you don't want to eat,
that's fine but maybe you'll change your mind.''

She didn't wait for Brenna to agree but got up and
went over to the refrigerator. While she was rum-
maging around in it, Brenna turned on the TV.

''I'm just going to see if they have anything—''

"Good idea."

But the only news she could find was on the weather channel and that was just about the storm. After all, it was only one plane down and with only one man aboard. Hardly a major story. It would be on the evening news, no doubt, but until then she'd just have to wait.

"Shane has family in Virginia," Brenna said quietly. "They should be notified."

"I think Bob's taking care of that. Come and have some coffee."

Brenna went. As difficult as it was for her to admit, there was nothing else she could do. Nothing except wait.

And pray.

Chapter 8

Saturday

Consciousness returned slowly. He was aware first of smells that triggered a deep sense of danger, probably what dragged him back to awareness. He smelled aviation fuel, not the whiffs of it on the air that you caught crossing a tarmac, and that he'd always enjoyed. This was the heavy, ominous smell of spilled fuel, signaling that fire might not be far off.

He stirred and felt something holding him down. Real fear roared through him. To be trapped helpless in a fire— His hands fumbled, touched metal. An action performed uncounted thousands of times without thought becomes instinct. He found and undid the seat belt latch.

He heard it click but more than that, he heard wind.

Or was it his own breathing? He opened his eyes, shut them again instantly at the stabbing pain that went straight through his head, and then felt pain everywhere.

Everywhere. There wasn't an inch of him that didn't throb. Pain threatened to swallow him. He fought against it, fighting to stay aware, to think past the pain. If he gave in to it—

He'd crashed. That was it. His chopper had gone down. Dammit, the Iraqis would be after him. He had to find cover, had to wait for the recon teams to locate him, sleep by day, signal by night, he knew the drill, had practiced it often enough....

His eyes opened again. The fog in his mind began to clear. He wasn't in Iraq. That was years ago. He was in Alaska. He'd iced over, flown into a temperature inversion and lost control of his aircraft. He was down and the plane—

Slowly, Shane struggled to sit up. Incredibly, he was still in his pilot's chair. There were even fragments of the cockpit around him but they were just that, fragments. The roof of the plane looked as though it had been peeled back by a can opener, the walls on either side were gone, everything was twisted and broken.

And still he smelled the fuel—

Quickly, despite the pain that chewed at him, he eased himself out of the chair. The plane was lying at a slight angle but basically upright. He half pulled, half dragged himself out of the shattered fuselage. The landing gear had sheared off on impact. He wasn't more than five feet off the ground.

Without stopping to think, he let go and dropped. The scream that tore from him echoed off the distant hills. Mother of God, his leg must have been broken. If it hadn't, it sure as hell was now. Prone on the ground, wondering if he was ever going to be able to move again, he touched his left leg gingerly. Just above the knee, he could feel the telltale bulge of bone jutting out.

Great. Down and crippled. This was turning into one hell of a day.

Okay, think it through. Control the pain, don't let it control you. Having a broken leg changed things some but not all that much. He still had to get whatever gear he could out of the plane.

He flew with the standard survival issue, flares, radio, basic first aid stuff, thermal blankets, and so on. It wasn't the kind of stuff he thought about much but now it meant the difference between life and death.

He had no idea how cold it was but for sure it was well below freezing. It would be dark soon and colder still. If he didn't get some sort of shelter rigged up fast, this whole exercise was going to get very academic very fast.

There was just the small matter of not being able to stand. Fine, okay, he could still crawl. Inch by agonizing inch, he worked his way over to a gap in what was left of the cabin toward the cockpit. Luck was with him for a change. The survival gear, contained within a bright orange pack, had been knocked loose from the locker and thrown to the ground. Sweat was dripping into his eyes and he was half blind with pain, but he got hold of the pack and managed to drag it away from the plane.

He got maybe ten yards before his strength gave out. The buzzing in his ears was becoming a roar. Something about plunging out of the sky, having his plane disintegrate around him and breaking a leg just wasn't working all that well for him.

"Getting soft," he murmured and laughed. Hell with it, he wasn't dead yet. He turned his face to the sky and shut his eyes for a moment. Snow fell softly; he felt it on his mouth like the gentlest kiss.

Not dead yet but he was going to be unless he hurried. First things first. He dug out the medical kit. Sure enough, it had several doses of morphine. The temptation to inject himself with just one was almost overwhelming but he knew what the price would be. The pain would ease up, he'd start to relax and without even knowing it, he'd fall asleep. And never wake.

They said freezing to death was a pretty easy way to go but Shane wasn't ready to find out yet. The morphine would have to wait. Right now, the sharp edge of pain was the best thing he had going for him. It spurred him to do what had to be done.

God bless the space program, he thought as he unrolled the tissue thin tent that contained its own support poles. NASA had come up with all sorts of incredible materials, and put them to incredible uses. One flick of the wrist and the thing sprang open. Granted, it was barely large enough for one person but he'd booked a single so that was fine.

He crawled in, spread one of the thermal blankets

on the bottom, and wrapped the other two around himself. By the time he finished, he was shivering uncontrollably. His hands shook so badly that he couldn't close his fingers around anything else in the pack. He needed to get out the radio, get out a signal to tell them he was still alive. He had to do that right away—

Blackness swam before his eyes. He had a moment to wonder if the broken leg was the extent of his injuries. Had he also hit his head? Was he feeling the effects of a concussion?

He tried to raise a hand, to feel any damage to his head, but the effort was beyond him. He slumped down on the floor of the survival tent, struggled to get up, failed and was finally still.

The wind whistled around the wreck. The snow thickened, falling over it, slowly but steadily hiding its shape. The sun ended its brief winter visit for one day and dipped below the horizon. Night fell.

"It's getting dark," Brenna said. Bob had called twice more, each time to reassure her yet again that everything was being done. She appreciated his words but listening between the lines she heard something different. Everything *would* be done as soon as the weather cleared and it was daylight. Until then, there wasn't anything anyone could do, not with the best will in the world.

After she spoke with him each time, Brenna gave the phone to Carol. She walked away, giving them some privacy to talk but even so, she couldn't help but be aware of Carol's growing tension. The last time her friend hung up the phone she looked truly stricken.

Turning to her now, Brenna said gently, "I wish you'd tell me."

Carol set her coffee cup down. Her hand shook slightly. "Tell you what?"

"You know, whatever it is Bob is telling you but not me."

"What makes you think—?"

"Come on. I know both of you. Just tell me, please."

Carol took a deep breath and closed her eyes for a moment. Softly, she said, "There hasn't been anything from Shane."

"Anything?"

"A radio signal." Quickly, Carol added, "There could be any number of explanations for that. The emergency radio in his survival pack might have something wrong with it. Or it could have been destroyed in the crash. Or the weather conditions might be wreaking havoc with the transmission."

"Or he might not be able to send a signal." Not if he was dead or so badly injured as to be the next thing to.

"They just don't know," Carol admitted. "Look, the rescue choppers will be airborne at first light. Even if the weather hasn't cleared, they're going to fly, you know that. They'll find him. After all, they've got his last position."

But it would be hours before they could reach him and meanwhile there was a storm raging. Even if he was alive, how could he possibly survive the night?

For a brief moment, Brenna wondered if she should be hoping for his sake that he was already dead.

"I think I'll have that coffee now," she said and went to get it.

Shane liked her coffee. He teased her about it being strong enough to get a dead man's heart going. He also claimed it was an aphrodisiac and he'd never missed an opportunity to prove it, not since that first time...

Two months earlier...

He had the most extraordinary chest. It looked as though it had been sculpted from marble, somehow brought to life, and very lightly dusted with golden hair.

"I thought pilots just sort of sat there," she said.

"I row."

She'd never take a boat for granted again. Her fingers traced a path down each of his heavily muscled arms. He was so extraordinarily male and the way he made her feel—as if she were losing herself and didn't even care.

He said something else, she replied, then said, "This is a nice couch but—" Her own daring amazed her. She was never like this, absolutely never.

"I have an even nicer bed."

"Do you really?" Who was this woman, this confident, flirtatious and decidedly lustful woman?

"You could decide for yourself."

But she already had and she said so.

He lifted her easily. She felt light, free, as though

the earth would never hold her again. The bedroom was in darkness. Shane lowered her onto the bed and flicked on a lamp.

"Better?" he asked.

She nodded, not quite trusting herself to speak. His eyes holding hers, he removed her blouse and skirt. A slow flush darkened her cheeks. His eyes swept over her. The light in them was utterly male and unmistakably possessive.

Knowing how she must look to him quickened her pulse. She hadn't been lying when she said lingerie was her secret vice. It—and books—were her only indulgences. She loved silken bikini panties, lacy teddies, embroidered garter belts and all the rest. Dressing for their date, she had chosen an apricot-hued bra that barely covered her nipples, matching panties that were little more than a thong, and a lacy garter belt that rode high on her hips. Attached to it were pale, lacy stockings that emphasized the long, slender length of her legs.

"Beautiful," Shane murmured. He dropped light, quick kisses along the exposed swell of her breasts, coming close to but not quite touching her nipples. Even so, they hardened so that the lacy fringe of the bra no long covered them. Shane smiled and passed his tongue over first one and then the other. The quiver that ran through Brenna could not be concealed.

"You are a very responsive woman," he said as he undid the front clasp of the bra and spread it open. His palms were calloused. Rubbing over her breasts, they were exquisitely abrasive.

"I think that may have more to do with you," she murmured. A hot, liquid weight was pooling between her thighs. She felt a desperate need to reach out to him, to end this, but restrained herself. Partly, she didn't think he would allow it but more she sensed where he was leading her and wanted to follow.

His mouth followed his hands. He circled each nipple with his tongue before sucking it slowly and strongly. The rhythm of his caress echoed deep within her. She twisted beneath him, clasping his hair between her fingers and moaned softly.

He raised his head. A dark flush stained his high-boned cheeks. "I really didn't want to rush this," he said thickly.

She was breathless, hardly able to respond. "You're not." Her hands went to his belt buckle, tugging urgently.

He left her briefly, mere seconds, but she was bereft. When he returned, nothing lay between them but the tiny scraps of her own clothes. He felt so good against her, his skin smooth and warm, stretched taut over powerful muscles and sinew. He moved with instinctive grace, this proud, intelligent man who made her laugh and filled the empty places within her which she had left ignored for far too long.

His erection, pressing against her, was long and thick. She reached down her hand, stroking him gently.

"Don't," he said, "please...I want..."

"I want, too," she said and continued stroking him.

He raised himself on his arms, his muscles corded, and gazed down into her eyes. Whatever he saw must have satisfied him. He slipped his fingers under the thin elastic on one side of her panties and with one sharp tug, snapped it. Baring her to him, he caressed the soft, moist folds of her womanhood.

Clad only in the garter belt and stockings, feeling more wanton than she would ever have imagined possible, she opened her legs. He entered her in a long, smooth motion that seemed endless. He was so very big that for a moment she wondered at her ability to accommodate him. But her body adjusted as though it had been waiting for him, and only him, all this time.

When he was fully settled within her, he moved again, slowly withdrawing, returning, withdrawing. The languorous strokes drove her to the edge. She gasped, her head tossing back and forth against the pillows. Her hips arched, drawing him even deeper within her.

His self-control was formidable. Even as a red mist of raw passion seized her, some tiny part of her consciousness realized this and marveled at it. Even as his chest rose and fell with the urgency of each breath and a fine sheen of perspiration glistened on his forehead, he waited, holding himself back, giving her everything.

Until there was no more she could take. The pressure building within her became overwhelming. She cried out, clasping him, as pleasure more intense than any she had ever imagined became all-consuming. With a fierce groan, he surrendered at last, pouring himself into her.

Saturday

Brenna set the coffee cup back down in the sink. Her hands were shaking too hard to hold it. She raised her head. In the kitchen window, she could see the reflection of a woman, pale and disembodied against the night. As she watched, tears slipped from the woman's eyes and slid soundlessly down her face, away into the darkness.

Chapter 9

Saturday

Shane moaned in his sleep. Something was wrong. It was...what exactly? He couldn't seem to wake up. The fog of unconsciousness clung to him with peculiar tenacity. He had to fight his way up as though from the bottom of a very deep, dark well.

Something was wrong. That single thought shone as a lone light against the obscurity that cloaked his mind. Clinging to it, he rose slowly to awareness.

He was cold. The furnace must be on the blink. He'd get up, check the thermostat, in just a second. Sleep tried to claim him again. He struggled against it.

Why couldn't he just wake up? He'd always been a light sleeper. In the Gulf War, his buddies joked

that he woke up when somebody coughed as far away
as in Tehran. That was okay with him; he'd never
needed much sleep. Now he seemed to be making up
for that.

Jeez, it really was cold. And his bed...what had
happened to his bed? How come the mattress was so
hard and lumpy all of a sudden?

Because it wasn't his bed. He wasn't in his apartment. He was on the ground. Downed.

His eyes shot open. He was instantly, painfully
awake. Very painfully. The burning agony in his leg
made him gasp. Slowly, he sat up. He was wrapped
in the survival blankets, inside the tent he'd had the
sense to set up, in what had turned out to be his last
moments of consciousness. If he hadn't, he'd be dead
by now.

But he wasn't. He was most definitely alive. No
one could possibly feel this much pain and not be
alive.

Okay, that was the good news. The bad news was
that life might still turn out to be a very short-term
condition.

He moved gingerly, pulling himself into a sitting
position. The effort made his mouth twist but he kept
at it until he was sitting more or less upright. The
walls of the tent gleamed dully around him. His own
body heat and the reflective, insulating fabric kept the
air temperature inside the tent somewhere in the low
sixties, he estimated. Outside, it would be a whole
different story.

The wind was howling. When he inched a hand
from beneath the blanket and lifted one edge of the

tent flap very slightly, all he could see was white. Snow was piled up all around him; he had no idea how deep. That meant it would also be piled up on whatever was left of his plane. Even if rescuers did get airborne any time soon, and even if they did have his correct coordinates, they were still going to have a hell of a time spotting him.

Taking a deep breath, struggling for control, he reached for the orange pack and pulled it closer to him. The radio was there. He hadn't imagined it. With a sigh of relief, he got it out and flicked the power switch.

Nothing happened.

Okay, no sweat. The batteries were probably jarred loose. He pried open the back of the radio and checked. There were batteries all right, but they didn't look loose. He'd changed the batteries himself just two weeks ago as part of routine survival gear maintenance—and he'd checked them before installing them, also routine—so he had no reason to think there was anything wrong with the batteries. That left the radio.

He put it up to his ear and shook it lightly. There was probably a name for that kind of very sophisticated technical testing, but he couldn't think of it just then. Inside the case, something rattled.

Shane frowned. Maracas were supposed to rattle, dice could rattle, baby toys could rattle. Radios were definitely not supposed to rattle.

So he'd fix it. Once he had enough light, he'd get the case off, take a look, figure out what was wrong and fix it. No problem. In the meantime, there were a few other things he needed to do. Answering nature's call in a survival tent wasn't easy, especially when it involved a little closer contact with subfreezing temperatures than he would normally have sought, but he managed. With so much snow, there'd be no lack of drinking water. That left the emergency rations.

Oh, boy, he remembered them from navy days. They had the virtue of making all the stuff you learned about eating worms and cockroaches sound like something you'd actually want to do. But with none of the insect world making itself available for fricasseeing, he had little choice. Unwrapping the indeterminable brown rectangle in the first package, he took a sniff. Somehow, it managed to smell like chocolate and beef jerky at the same time. Talk about a triumph of engineering.

It was also rock hard. He sighed and set to work on it. Chewing had never been tougher work. By the time he got to the point where he could actually swallow a piece of the stuff, he was beginning to think it was more trouble than it was worth. The only saving grace that he could think of was that it probably tasted so bad because it was so good for him. There had to be some direct relationship between the sheer unpalatability of the stuff and the proteins and carbohydrates packed into it. At least he sure hoped so.

Besides, having to concentrate all his strength and attention just on eating kept him from thinking about his leg. The pain hadn't lessened, not at all, but the shock of its mere existence was gone. Already, he couldn't quite remember what it felt like to not hurt.

He reached a hand down very carefully and let his fingers just brush against his leg. That was stupid, very, very stupid. The pain, like a ferocious monster that hadn't been paying full attention, awoke suddenly and howled inside him. Shane gasped. He snatched his hand back as though flames had licked it. Several moments passed before the pain began to subside again.

He didn't need any more lessons to tell him what was happening. His leg was broken, the bone protruding almost all the way through the skin. In addition, the surrounding area was becoming infected. He set the emergency rations aside and dug out the medical pack. Once again, he lingered over the morphine before rejecting it. Morphine wouldn't get the radio fixed.

He found the syringe prefilled with antibiotics and injected himself. Nowadays, he couldn't count absolutely on whatever was causing the infection to fall to the antibiotic. Too many germs were resistant. But he'd hope for the best.

That done, he settled back and thought about what to do next. He was still thinking about it when sleep caught him unawares.

Brenna raised her head. She was sitting on the couch. A book lay open in her lap but she had absolutely no idea what it was. She'd been drifting for several minutes, her thoughts silenced, her mind open and still.

What was that, just now? Had she actually heard something or was it her imagination? For just a moment, she could have sworn Shane was there with her, not doing or saying anything, just there.

Wishful thinking, that was all it was, and she wasn't about to let herself give in to it. If nothing else, she had to keep a firm grip on reality.

And the reality was that it was night. Carol was in the kitchen, making another pot of coffee. Bob had last called about an hour before. It was what he didn't say that mattered most. They still hadn't heard from Shane.

She swallowed hard against the tightness of her throat and stood up. Her whole body ached. Just then, she realized how tensely she was holding herself, as though in instant readiness.

For what? There was nothing she could do—except think and worry. And regret.

If only they hadn't argued....

Were there any more painful words in the English language than *if only?* She doubted it. How many people over how many eons had wished desperately that they could take back some word or action? Probably everyone who had ever lived.

And now she was one of them. People said there was safety in numbers but Brenna found none, at least not safety from the pain that enveloped her. The ordinary world, the one she hadn't been so foolish as to take for granted, was still out there somewhere. But she felt separated from it by an invisible force that entirely surrounded her and cut her off from the existence she had known only a few short hours before. The pain—and the regret—imprisoned her. They controlled every moment, every thought and every breath.

And there was no escape from them.

Brenna moved suddenly, as though trying to prove she could escape. But it was no use. She couldn't run away from this and if she had to sit still a moment longer, she truly thought she would go mad.

She turned, staring absently at the front door, only to realize that something had changed. All evening, she'd listened to the sound of sleet pelting against the door, the walls of the house, the windows. Now there was only silence.

Going over to the door, she opened it. Bitter cold hit her hard. She took a step back but continued to stare out for several moments. Finally unable to bear the freezing air any longer, she pushed the door shut. She was trembling all over, her lungs burning from the cold, but she also felt considerably more alive and energized than she had all evening.

Carol looked up as she came into the kitchen. "Was that the door I heard?"

Brenna nodded. "I opened it for a second. The sleet has stopped. It's snowing now."

"Hard?"

"Not too badly. We've seen worse, for sure. Look, I'm thinking of going out to the airport. You can stay here if you'd like. That would probably be better than trying to get home."

"Brenna—"

"I just can't sit here anymore. I'm afraid I'm really going to lose it if I do. At least at the airport, I'll know what's going on."

Carol came over and put her hands on her shoulders. Gently, she said, "Nothing's going on, honey. It can't until there's light."

"They might hear from Shane. If I'm there, I could talk with him."

Carol didn't reply but Brenna could see what was in her eyes. Quickly, she added, "They will hear from him, I know it."

"And when they do, Bob will call you immediately."

"I know but I want to be there. I can't just sit here."

Carol was clearly unconvinced. She started to say something else, thought better of it and sighed. "Okay, I understand. But I'm coming with you and I think we should take my car. This isn't the best time for you to be driving."

"It's not great out there," Brenna acknowledged. "I don't want you to take any more chances than you did coming over here."

"What chances? I just closed my eyes and let the car find the way." Carol grinned.

So did Brenna, shakily. "And you think we'd be better with you driving?"

"Hey, I got here, didn't I? Seriously, if you go, I'm going and it sure doesn't make any sense to take two cars."

"You're a good friend," Brenna said softly and went to get their coats.

Chapter 10

The airport blazed with lights. Walking into the main terminal, Brenna blinked hard. The fluorescent glare seemed to go right through her eyes to the back of her head. She glanced around nervously.

The few people to be seen were slumped in chairs, some asleep and the others looking as though they'd like to be that way. All flights were canceled because of the storm. A handful of weary airline employees kept vigil at otherwise empty counters.

Upstairs, it was a different story. Bob met them at the thick metal door marked Authorized Personnel Only. Beyond it was the corridor that led to the control tower and the various offices adjacent to it.

He nodded when he saw them. "How are the roads?"

"Not too bad," Carol said. "All things considered." They shared a quick hug.

Bob's face was strained. He looked exhausted and deeply worried but he managed a smile for Brenna. "Everyone's been briefed, the search patterns are all set. The guys are trying to get a little rest, but come first light, they'll be right at it."

"Have you heard anything?" she asked. His reassurances were very kind but this was the heart of it.

Bob hesitated. Shane was his friend, too.

"Nothing yet but that doesn't mean much. He knows we can't do anything before light so maybe he just decided to hold off."

Carol cast her husband a quick look. That was ridiculous and they all knew it. There was no way Shane would wait to tell them he was alive just because the rescuers couldn't take off right away. Brenna knew if Bob was reaching that far, he must be even more worried than he was letting on.

"Do you have a pretty fair idea of where he went down?" Brenna asked. Forcing herself to put it that way—went down—hurt but she refused to hide from it.

"Absolutely. Shane gave the tower his coordinates and then confirmed them. We know where he is...well, within a general area."

They had reached the room next to the tower that was being used by the rescue effort. It was the same sort of all-purpose room that could be found in every office building, university, government institution and the like. The walls were beige, the ceiling laid with acoustic tile, the floor covered with a brown carpet that looked as though it had been picked for its sheer toughness. The furniture consisted of two large tables set at right angles with folding chairs set up around them. Maps were spread out on the tables. Several clipboards with printouts attached to them were scattered around. Brenna picked one up.

It took her a moment to realize what she was looking at. The printout was a transcription of a conversation. The last conversation between Shane and the control tower. Her eyes scanned it compulsively.

He declared an emergency, talked briefly with the tower, they mentioned an air field forty-five minutes away. It all seemed so calm, so matter-of-fact. And then—

Aleut 949: Roger, Anchorage Tower, doesn't look like an option. I'm coming down now.

Tower: Understood, Aleut 949.

Tower: Confirm course heading, Aleut 949.

So calm...

At the bottom of the page were two final lines of print:

Aleut 949: Anchorage Tower, Aleut 949, going down.

Tower: Roger, Aleut 949, we comp, air rescue will be notified, good luck.

And a note that radio transmission was breaking up at the point.

Brenna dropped the clipboard onto the table. She felt sick. Her first thought that she was going to have to find a bathroom or risk vomiting in front of everyone. But the sensation lessened. She sat down slowly.

"You okay?" Bob asked. He and Carol looked up from the maps they'd been studying.

Brenna nodded. She wasn't but there was no point

going into that. Too late, she realized that she had only just now fully accepted what was happening. When she was still at home, there had been an air of unreality about it all. That was gone.

"I'm going to get a weather update," Bob said. "Why don't you come with me and meet the guys?"

She agreed at once, grateful for the chance to do something...anything. Although the airport was shut down, the tower was far from quiet. At least a dozen people were clustered there, talking among themselves, some on telephones. They broke off as she entered with Bob.

"This is Brenna O'Hare," he said quietly.

It seemed no further explanation was necessary. They nodded, smiled gently, those closest to her reached out for a pat on the back or a touch on the arm. She murmured hello but really had nothing else to say. They knew why she was there but there was really no reassurance they could give her, or themselves for that matter.

Bob spoke with a young man in front of a computer screen. "How's it looking, George?"

"Good and bad. The storm's blowing out, be over in a couple more hours. But then there's this." He gestured to what looked to Brenna like a swirling mass of green with pockets of deep blue and red to the left of his screen.

"How long?" Bob asked.

"Hard to say. It's been a slow mover, we could have twenty-four, maybe even thirty-six hours. On the other hand, it's picked up some in just the last hour or two so it could get here a whole lot sooner."

"Another storm?" Brenna asked.

Bob nodded. "It could still miss us, right, George?"

The weatherman glanced up at them. His gaze settled on Brenna. "Sure," he said gently. "It could still miss."

But it wouldn't. He was sure of that, even though he wouldn't say it, and so was she. There was going to be a window—a day, maybe a day and a half long—during which they would have to find Shane. After that, the next storm would hit and all hope might well be lost.

Presuming, of course, that there was any hope to begin with.

But there had to be, didn't there? Where there was life, there was hope.

Where there was life—

Two months earlier

Brenna stirred slowly. She was waking from the most astounding dream. Fragments of it still drifted through her mind. Her cheeks warmed. She turned over, nestling deeper under the covers. Eyes still closed, she smiled. She didn't remember her dreams very often but she doubted she'd ever forget this one. Apparently, she had a whole lot better imagination than she'd thought.

For instance, right now she imagined she could feel something very warm and hard beside her. Something breathing slowly and steadily.

Something?

Her eyes flew open. Too startled to move, she stared at the thick mane of golden hair on the pillow beside her.

She didn't have golden hair. Far gone as she was, totally befuddled, she still knew she was brunette.

Shane had hair the shade of heavy, old gold lit by a rising sun.

Oh, right, Shane. She remembered him now. Extremely well.

Not some delightful figment of her imagination, after all, but a flesh-and-blood breathing man stretched out in bed sound asleep beside her. But then why shouldn't he be? It was his bed.

Last night, she had...they had...

She pressed her lips tight together, the better to let no astonished yelp sneak out, and slowly worked her way over to the far side of the bed. Without taking her eyes off him, she slid out from under the covers. Cool air touched her skin, making her shiver.

Which was hardly surprising considering that she was clad only in a silk garter belt and stockings.

Blushing beet red, stunned by the evidence of her own wantonness, she plucked an extra blanket from the foot of the bed and wrapped it around herself. The rest of her clothes lay on various parts of the floor. She scooped them up and tiptoed out of the room.

In the bathroom, she dressed quickly, splashed a little cold water on her face, and ran her fingers through her hair. None of that left her feeling even slightly better to face the day, but then she hadn't really expected it to.

He had picked her up the previous evening. That

left her with no way of getting home unless she called a taxi. Or woke him.

She hesitated. Just sneaking out without a word was not an option. If a man did that to her, she'd be hurt and angry. She was willing to assume that Shane had the same capacity for feeling.

On the other hand, waking him meant coming face-to-face with her own feelings.

She was standing uncertainly in the living room when the matter was settled for her.

"Are you always such an early riser?" Shane asked.

Brenna turned so quickly that she snagged a toe on the thick plush rug and almost pitched over headfirst. Catching herself just in time, she also caught him smiling.

Easy for him. He wasn't standing there, feeling acutely awkward, wearing yesterday's clothes. In fact, he wasn't wearing any clothes at all. Looking him up and down as she did—and she couldn't seem to stop herself—she didn't spot so much as a fig leaf.

But then fig leaves were probably hard to come by in Alaska, even during mild winters.

"I didn't mean to wake you," she said. "Well, actually, I thought maybe I should because I didn't feel right just leaving but then I thought you might be tired and it would be rude to wake you so I really wasn't sure what I should do and—"

"Shhh," he said. He crossed the room, his body gleaming darkly in the light filtering through the curtains. He was tall and lithe, the embodiment of male power and beauty. Brenna stood frozen in place, feeling an instinct to retreat and yet utterly unable to take a step.

His hand caressed the length of her back. "There's nothing to be nervous about."

"I'm not n-nervous."

"You're an extraordinary woman." He applied very light pressure at the base of her spine, drawing her toward him.

"You're not so bad yourself."

"Shucks, ma'am, you keep that up and I'm liable to blush."

"I'd like to see that," Brenna murmured. "Something tells me you don't embarrass all that easily."

"Why, whatever could have given you that impression?"

She could feel the warmth of his skin through her thin blouse and skirt. The remembered scent of him clung to her. Her senses swam. Without thought, she reached out and grasped his shoulders.

"It's all right," he murmured. His mouth on hers, he tasted and teased, his tongue thrusting, withdrawing, thrusting again until she moaned with the sheer frustrating delight of it all.

He laughed then—a deep, male sound of triumph—and drew her hard against his nakedness. She felt his strength tempered by control, and trembled. When he drew her down onto the floor, she was beyond even the thought of protest.

Chapter 11

Sunday

He woke to light. Opening his eyes slowly, Shane lay unmoving for several minutes. He realized at once what the light meant—it was day. He had survived the night. But he had to muster his strength before he could do much with that.

Finally, he managed to draw himself up into a half-sitting position and ease the tent flap open just enough to see out. Luck looked to be with him, for a change. He was not, as he had half expected, buried in snow. Perhaps a foot's accumulation surrounded the tent.

Not far away, he could see where the wind had formed drifts six and more times that high. It had done the same around the wreckage of his plane. Because he knew where it was, he could still make out the vague shape of what had been an aircraft. But to just about anyone else, it would look like a mound of snow, nothing more.

And more snow was still coming down, although much lighter than it had been. It looked as though the storm had just about blown itself out.

More luck.

Okay, he was alive, the weather looked to be improving soon, and he needed to get his act together in one hell of a hurry. The odds were that even with his coordinates—assuming they were actually correct—he was going to be very tough to spot from the air. The least he could do was give his rescuers a little help.

He fished out the radio and using the small assortment of tools that were also part of the survival gear, he managed to get the back of it off. Peering inside, he cursed softly. The thing had taken a harder hit than he'd wanted to believe. It looked as though some of the soldering was cracked. If that was the case, he had no hope of getting the radio to work.

But he wasn't about to give up. As a kid, he'd spent endless summer vacations messing around with all sorts of electronics. Heck, once he'd managed to get a shortwave radio he'd built to pick up Moscow. At least, Mr. Blansky from down the street said it was Moscow when he came over to translate. He also said the Communists were filthy pigs and told Shane the proudest boast any man could ever make was to say he was free.

Good old Mr. Blansky. Shane hadn't thought of him in years. He'd been right, though. Freedom was what it was all about. And right now Shane's best hope of freedom—not to say his only hope—lay in getting the radio going again.

Slowly, moving painstakingly so as to not cause any more damage, he eased the battery case out and took a look at the leads underneath. Didn't look too bad. Now for the rest of it—

Twenty minutes later, Shane sat back and wiped the sweat from his forehead. He thought he'd found two loose connections where a couple of small boards plugged in and managed to fix them. If he was right, he'd know in a minute.

Cautiously, he switched the radio on. The burst of static that followed immediately was just about the sweetest music he'd ever heard.

"Anything?" Bob asked.

Carl shook his head. He was another youngish man Brenna had met during the long night. Carl was on radio. He was tall, skinny, pale and seemed to have been born with headphones permanently connected to his ears. At some point, Bob had told her in an aside that Carl was a former Navy sonar man. He was said to be able to distinguish the sounds made by different pods of dolphins hundreds of miles away, and correctly identify their individual members by name. Although the value of that skill in the Navy meant absolutely nothing to her, it was apparently a very well respected skill.

Too bad none of that helped right now.

"Nothing," Carl said. "Frequency's cold."

"Keep trying."

He nodded, eyes glued to his transmitter.

Outside, light was breaking through the still-thick clouds. Brenna counted four small choppers on the runway, ready for takeoff. She could hear the air controllers giving their clearance.

Officially, the airport was still closed. Weary would-be travelers remained stranded in the terminals. The rescue craft had priority and besides, their pilots had made it clear they weren't willing to wait any longer.

The men had appeared with mugs of thick coffee in their hands, a night's growth of beard shadowing their faces, and eyes red-rimmed from the scant sleep they'd managed to snatch on cots. They knew and respected Shane, but even if they hadn't, they would have been there. It was what they did.

She watched as the first chopper took off. Barely had it lifted off the runway than the next followed, and so on until all four were airborne. Even after they disappeared into the clouds, Brenna stayed at the window, wishing there was some way she could send her prayers with them.

A burst of static made her turn around. Even as she did so, she realized that everyone in the tower had heard it, too.

John Dieter, a big, middle-aged man with the body of a linebacker who was heading up the rescue effort, spoke for them all.

"Carl?"

The radioman didn't answer at once. He had the headphones pressed to his ears. His concentration was intense. Slowly, he put his hands down. "I don't know. I thought maybe I heard something but—"

"Keep listening."

He did for several more moments but finally they all had to admit that there was nothing. "Could be interference from the weather," Carl said.

"Is that likely?" Brenna asked Bob.

He shrugged. "It happens, unfortunately. You know how you pick up certain TV stations sometimes but not others?"

"I've seen that."

"The same thing happens with radio reception. Heavy clouds, lightning, sunspots, heck, just about anything affects it. Sometimes, I think it's a miracle it works at all."

He saw in her face what she thought of that and backtracked quickly. "Not that radios aren't reliable—they are. It's just that there could be problems depending on the terrain, the atmospherics, things like that."

"So it was just static?"

"That just means some kind of electrical discharge. It can be caused naturally or there could be something on the frequency and we just can't make it out."

"Something?"

He looked at her gently. "It wasn't enough, honey. I wish to God that it was, but it wasn't. We've just got to be patient."

She tried hard not to let him see how disappointed she was, but she didn't think she managed it. The pilots, airborne now, began to call in. They would be over the site where Shane was believed to have gone down in a couple of hours.

Until then, there was nothing to do but wait.

"Maybe you should try to get some rest," Carol suggested. She looked worn out herself, but she smiled for her friend and gave her a hug.

Blinking back tears, Brenna said, "You know, I don't think I've told you and Bob how grateful I am to have such good friends."

"You'd do the same for us. Besides, we care for Shane, too."

Brenna nodded. She was painfully aware that Carol and Bob didn't know that she and Shane had argued. They had no idea what had been said, or how angry he'd been when he left. She couldn't bear to tell them. The hurt and guilt were just too much.

"Maybe I will lie down for a while," she said. As truly as she appreciated what they were doing, she needed some time to be by herself. The check she was keeping on her emotions was becoming intolerable. She was desperately afraid it was about to crack.

The cots were set up in a small room next to the lockers. It was dark in there and very quiet. She found a pillow and blankets, took off her shoes and laid down.

She didn't really think she'd be able to sleep, and wasn't sure she would have wanted to anyway. Asleep, she might dream. It was better to lie awake in the quiet room, her arms folded under her head, looking up at the ceiling.

Better, that is, until she realized that while she

might be able to stave off dreams, she could not escape memories.

Two months before

The shower was strong and hot. Water flowed over her, falling in droplets off her hardened nipples, running in rivulets down the length of her body. Eyes closed, Brenna moaned softly. Shane stood directly behind her. She felt his hardness against the small of her back. His hands, wet and slick, moved over her breasts, along the slightly rounded curve of her abdomen to her thighs.

She tried to turn, needing desperately to touch him, but he wouldn't allow it. Held immobile, she could do nothing to resist the rapturous sensation that followed his touch. His fingers stroked the silken folds of her womanhood, probing lightly, enticing but never remotely satisfying. The need he provoked consumed her. There was nothing except his hard, powerful body, his possessive touch and the heat swirling all around and through her.

He took hold of her hips, moving her against him, controlling her for his pleasure and her own. A tiny flare of resentment ignited within her. It faded when a groan broke from him.

With a flick of his wrist, he turned off the water. In almost the same motion, he lifted her. A rack just outside the shower held thick white bath sheets. Shane took one and began to dry her. She grasped his hands, stopping him.

"Not now," Brenna whispered. Standing on tiptoe,

she took his mouth with hers, eating at it, desperate to have all of him. He lifted her high against him, holding her, and wrapped her legs around his hips. Like that, he carried her into the bedroom.

The bed was still in disarray from the night before. Shane sat down on the edge and let himself fall back so that she straddled him. Surprised, and delighted, Brenna didn't hesitate. She took hold of him with one hand and guided him into her.

Immediately, he thrust hard and deep, claiming her completely. Her eyes closed as she trembled on the very edge of ecstasy. Her inner muscles tightened. She rose until she was balanced on his smooth, hot tip, held herself there for an exquisite instant, then slowly lowered herself onto his full length, inch by enthralling inch.

His hands clenched into fists but he made no attempt to stop her, or to retake control of their love-making. The freedom he gave her made Brenna feel more than slightly delirious. She had never known such complete liberation of the senses. Her hands caressed his heavily muscled chest, feeling the ragged harshness of his life's breath just beneath her touch. She marveled at so much power beneath and in her, held in such check. Rising once more, she slowly lowered herself again onto his hard, thick length.

"Enjoying yourself?" His voice was deep and roughened by passion. His eyes gleamed dangerously.

Holding herself still, Brenna braced her hands on his shoulders. She ignored the predator light of his gaze and smiled. "Oh, yes, can't you tell?"

He made a sound very much like a growl. She half

expected him to take control then and end it but he surprised her. Raising his hips slightly, he made a half-twisting motion that moved him suddenly even more deeply within her.

And when he did—

Brenna cried out, a thread of sound, startled, breathless as the power he had kept in check so long was suddenly and most delightfully released.

Chapter 12

Sunday

Shane put the radio down slowly. His hand ached from gripping it for so long. Giving up was repugnant to him but even he had to admit that the damn thing just wasn't working. For over an hour, he had been trying to transmit. So far as he could tell, nothing had gotten through. For sure, nothing had come back.

There were several possible explanations. The radio simply might not be working. He had no way of knowing for sure that he'd fixed it. Or perhaps he had and it was working fine but the weather was messing up reception. Whichever was the case, he was in the same spot as when he'd started.

Except that the pain in his leg was worse. While he was busy with the radio, he'd been able to ignore everything else. But the moment he put it down and slumped back on the floor of the survival tent, he knew he was in trouble.

He was due for another shot of the antibiotic but judging by what he could feel, the first one hadn't done much good. The pain in his leg was worse, a sure sign that the infection was spreading. Still, it wasn't as though he had a whole lot of choice. He found another of the syringes and injected himself. Yet again, he glanced at the morphine and yet again he rejected it.

Now that he was no longer concentrating on the radio, he realized that he was feverish. Morphine would only make it harder—if not impossible—for him to keep his wits about him. Instead, he took a couple of analgesics.

When that was done, he forced himself to eat more of the emergency rations. His stomach threatened to rebel but he managed to keep a small amount down. Figuring he'd better not press his luck, he decided to leave the rest for later. Lying back, he found as comfortable a position as he could manage and let his thoughts drift.

He couldn't remember a time when he hadn't wanted to fly. It seemed to have been a part of his life always. And if it ended up also being the means of his death, he'd have to just accept that. But he wasn't ready to die yet, not by a long shot. A grim smile twisted his mouth. But hell, right now it hurt to be alive!

The pain subsided a little when he let his mind go free. When he let it return to other, happier times.

Maybe it was the fever, or just the sensation of being more utterly alone than he'd ever been in his life, but it seemed as though the memories were more vivid, more real than any he had ever known. And they all seemed to have to do with Brenna....

Two months earlier

The building was cookie-cutter institutional, no better or worse than dozens Shane had seen all over the world. Late afternoon and already dark, lights blazed from every window. People came and went singly and in groups. They seemed in high spirits. Whatever they did inside, they enjoyed it.

He checked his watch just as the second hand swept by 5:00 p.m. precisely. Punctuality was second nature for him, even before he joined the military. He was faintly suspicious of people who couldn't turn up on time.

Brenna had given him directions. He followed them easily to the third floor, south wing, and found himself standing in front of what looked like a good-size lab. Several people inside were just putting on their coats. Others were still at work.

"Excuse me," he said.

A young man turned his way. "May I help you?"

May I? Seemed like they grew them polite *and* educated around here.

"I'm looking for Ms. O'Hare."

The young man raised an eyebrow ever so slightly. "You mean Dr. O'Hare?"

Doctor? Okay, he'd missed that but then she hadn't seen fit to mention it, either.

"Guess I do," he said.

"Through there."

Shane nodded his thanks. He ignored the surreptitious glances coming his way and headed for a smaller lab set off from the larger one. Brenna was there, sitting on a stool with her back to him. She was peering into a microscope. Not wanting to break her concentration, he waited. After several moments, she jotted something down in a notebook beside her, straightened up and rubbed the back of her neck.

He took that opportunity to knock lightly on the open door.

She turned, saw him and smiled. He smiled back. They stood like that, just smiling at each other, until Brenna laughed a little selfconsciously and got off the stool.

"Right on time," she said.

"That's me. How's your work going?"

"Fine. It's pretty routine at this stage. I just need to put a couple of things away."

He nodded and watched as she moved around the lab, covering several instruments, securing trays of specimens. She was such a naturally graceful woman. It was a pleasure to watch her. Of course, it was a pleasure to do other things, too.

"Something funny?" she asked, catching sight of his expression.

"Not exactly. I guess you could just say I feel...happy."

He did, too, and it startled him a little to realize it.

He had a good life, one that involved lots of hard work but that was fine. He was proud of his accomplishments and satisfied with the place he'd made for himself. He certainly didn't think of himself as being unhappy. But happiness wasn't something he'd really gone after. It seemed frivolous somehow, not really grown-up.

He'd have to reconsider that now.

Brenna had that look on her face that a woman got when she was touched. That made him feel even better. He wasn't exactly tops in the sensitivity department but he seemed to have done all right this time.

"That's nice," she said softly. "I'm glad to hear it."

He shrugged, hoping they weren't going to have some big discussion about it. He should have known better. Brenna was a smart woman, too. She knew the worth of silence.

"Hungry?" she asked.

"Starved. A certain lady of my acquaintance dangled a steak in front of me."

"She didn't! The tease. What did you do?"

"Took her up on it, of course."

"Then I guess she better deliver." Plucking her coat from a hook by the door, Brenna flipped the light off. As they exited through the larger lab, she said good-night to the others still there. It seemed to Shane that every step they took was followed by half a dozen pairs of eyes. Barely had they reached the hallway when the low murmur of voices started.

"Would I be wrong to think you don't usually get picked up for a date here?" he asked.

"You're the first."

He stopped for a second, holding her lightly by the arm. "Should I be flattered?"

She looked right at him. Her eyes were filled with good humor and more—intelligence, gentleness, strength. She was one hell of a woman.

Without warning, she stepped closer and kissed him hard. Against his mouth, she murmured, "You damn well better be."

They went to Brenna's house. Shane followed in his car. She drove confidently and capably, just the way he expected. When they got inside, he asked if she'd like any help in the kitchen.

"Why don't you get the woodstove going instead?" she suggested. "Then come keep me company."

He fed kindling into the stove, lit it and added a few larger pieces. When the fire was going well, he stood for a moment, glancing around the room. Not for the first time, he was struck by the comfort it offered. The furniture was pleasant without being ostentatious. There were plenty of books, some actually on shelves others stacked neatly under end tables. The pictures on the walls and the few knickknacks scattered around weren't some decorator's idea of good taste. They looked like originals by folk artists, people who maybe hadn't been "discovered" yet but who cared about what they did. Compared to his own place, Brenna's house was an actual home. He caught himself envying her that just a little.

"Everything all right?" she asked when he came into the kitchen. It was the short arm of an L that led right off the living room. The same warm feeling continued there. A collection of pots that looked well used hung from wrought iron hooks above the stove. There were cookbooks at one end of the counter next to an earthenware pot filled with dry flowers.

Brenna was turning on the broiler. He caught sight of the steaks on a nearby cutting board and grinned.

"Hey, I thought we were having dinner alone."

"Too much?"

"Not if four more people are coming over. Are they?"

"I hate to disappoint you but it's just us."

"I'll bear up."

"You do that," she said and handed him a corkscrew. "How about picking out a bottle of wine while you're at it?"

She had a small but good selection on a wine rack under the counter. He chose a Washington state burgundy he'd had before and uncorked it. Just as he finished, his nose twitched.

Brenna was slicing onions. She had a skillet on top of the stove with butter melting in it.

His eyes widened. "Fried onions?"

"What's steak without them?"

"A woman with looks, brains, a sense of humor *and* she fries onions? I've died and gone to heaven."

"Not quite yet but it could happen."

He grinned. "Oh, really? And just how did you plan on accomplishing that?"

She put the knife she'd been wielding down, sidled up real close to him, and said, "I've got the ultimate weapon." Her tongue touched the curve of his jaw, sending a lightning jolt of pleasure through him. "Baked potatoes *with* sour cream."

"You realize we're going to have to work this off?"

"It'll be tough."

"In fact..." His hands slipped round to cup her buttocks. "Maybe it would be a good idea to start now."

"Sort of a preemptive work off?"

"You could put it that way." He reached behind her and turned off the burner under the skillet. "Besides, steaks should be cooked at room temperature."

"Oooh, those are still icy cold."

"Bad, very bad."

She slid her fingers through his hair and moved against him slowly, tantalizingly. "How long do you think they need?"

He drew her into the circle of his arms. His mouth traced a leisurely path down her throat. "Hours."

"Hours?"

"Can't rush steaks."

She leaned back slightly so that her gaze met his. Her eyes were wide and dark. "Really?"

"Oh, yeah," he said, his voice caressing, his hands following. "Definitely hours."

Sunday

Seemed like Shane could still taste those steaks. He and Brenna had gotten around to eating them eventually and they were the best steaks he'd ever had. Of course, that might have had something to do with eating them in a bed still warm from frenzied lovemaking, feeding each other bits as they sipped wine and laughed over nothing in particular.

It was so good with Brenna, and not just the sex, spectacular though that was. It was all good—the talking and laughing, the silences and the looking forward. He'd never done that with a woman before, looking forward to a future that might include them together, wondering what it might be like, maybe even starting to plan it a little.

But he had with Brenna.

Damn her.

Chapter 13

Sunday

If she drank any more coffee, she'd be sick. Brenna put the plastic cup down and looked at the wall clock. It was two minutes past the last time she'd looked at it. In two more minutes, when she checked again— She sighed and rubbed her eyes wearily. Her head throbbed but she barely noticed it. All her attention was focused on the agonizingly slow passage of minutes.

Carl glanced up, saw her and said softly, "Half hour or so now."

She managed a weak smile. "Thanks."

In half an hour, the rescue choppers would reach the location where Shane was believed to have gone down. It was very likely that she would know something soon. The thought of what that might be was terrifying. She knew she might need all her strength. The problem was that she had no idea if it would be enough.

Years after her father was killed, she remembered her mother saying that at the moment when she opened the front door and saw the two police officers standing there, she'd had the terrible wish that she could just stop time. There was a part of her that would have chosen never to have to go on to the next moment, to hear the words spoken, the fear made fact, the pain unleashed.

Brenna finally knew what she meant. It would almost have been better to be frozen in some unending present than to have to move on into a future that held the promise for such anguish.

Almost.

She looked at the clock again. This time, she'd made it through three minutes. It was a very small victory but she took what she could get.

Several more people came into the tower. The airport had reopened a short time before. A few planes had taken off and several more had landed but far more remained. The new arrivals spoke with John Dieter, who despite the long night looked tough and alert. Once, they glanced in her direction.

"FAA," Bob murmured. He had come up beside her. "They just got in."

"They investigate crashes."

"That's right. They'll be here for the duration."

"They try to figure out who's to blame, don't they?"

"Who or what."

"You don't think—" The sudden possibility that Shane might be held responsible for what had happened, and might not be able to defend himself, hit her hard. "They wouldn't say that—"

"Easy, honey," Bob said. "We already know what caused this. It hurts like hell but the plain fact is Shane drew just about the worst cards a pilot can get. Nobody could have predicted that weather front would move like it did. Situations like that are incredibly rare—thank God—but when they happen, a plane gets caught in the wrong place at the wrong time, and there just isn't a whole lot anyone can do."

"You're saying this all came down to luck?" The thought horrified her. Life shouldn't depend on anything so capricious.

"I wish it didn't but sometimes—" Bob shrugged. His eyes were red-rimmed, he looked exhausted. She remembered how much he liked Shane, not just as a boss but as a friend.

"Hey, don't listen to me. I'm just tired. Look, Shane's the best damn pilot there is. With the kind of skill he's got, he can take an end run around the worst luck that ever came down the pike. Luck, schmuck, my money's on him."

Brenna managed a weary smile back but her heart wasn't in it. She kept thinking how grimly matter-of-fact the men from the FAA looked, as though there were nothing left to do except the paperwork.

Please God, don't let that be true.

Please—

There as a burst of static over the radio. The tension

in the room jumped so suddenly that it seemed to bong off the walls.

"Anchorage Tower, this is Rescue one-four-six, repeat Rescue one-four-six. Come in."

John Dieter took the mike from Carl. "Rescue one-four-six, this is Anchorage Tower, say position."

"Roger, Anchorage Tower, this is Rescue one-four-six, we are at the coordinates. Established half-mile radius search area. Nothing so far."

"Say again, Rescue one-four-six."

"Roger, we are in position, visibility's good. Nothing yet."

"We comp, Rescue one-four-six. Tower out."

In the silence that followed, the men gathered in the control tower looked at one another. Quietly, Dieter said, "Nothing."

Bob repeated it. "Nothing."

"They just got there," Carol said.

Bob nodded. "Yeah, they just got there."

"Frank said visibility's good," Dieter said.

"How tough could it be to spot—" someone else chimed in.

"Even with the snow last night—"

"I mean, you gotta figure—"

"Figure what?" Brenna demanded. "What does this mean. Why don't they see anything?"

It fell to Bob to answer her. "We don't know. They did just get there, that's true. If the coordinates were off even slightly, they're going to have to widen the search area. And it did snow—"

"So you're saying that a crash site could be covered, hidden from view?" Brenna asked.

"It's possible," he admitted, "but there would have had to be several feet of snow, which could happen because of the wind and even so—"

"Frank's no tyro," Dieter said. "He knows how to read ground, covered or not. If there's a plane down there, he'll find it."

"And if there isn't—?" Brenna demanded.

"Then we'll expand the search area. We know what we're doing." More softly, Dieter added, "We've done it before."

One by one, the men nodded. Their faces were set, their expressions closed. They had to protect themselves, too, Brenna realized. They had done this before and would again, and without saying it, she knew that the outcomes were usually unhappy. They had to steel their own emotions against the sorrow that would otherwise overwhelm them.

But not this time. Oh, please, not this time.

She turned away quickly so they wouldn't see the tears that burned her eyes.

Carol put an arm around her shoulders. "Come and sit down, hon."

She let herself be led over to a chair and sat. Carol put a sweater around her shoulders. Only then did Brenna realize that she was shaking.

Long moments passed. This time she couldn't bear to look at the clock. Finally, the radio sprang to life again.

"Anchorage Tower, this is Rescue one-four-six, come in."

"Roger, Rescue one-four-six," Dieter said. "Go ahead."

"Expanding search area, going to one mile radius."

Quietly, almost to herself, Brenna said, "There's nothing there."

"That's why they're going to look over a wider distance," Carol agreed. "They'll find him."

Would they? There had been no radio signal and now no sign of the plane. Was it possible that it had been so destroyed on impact that the traces couldn't be spotted?

She couldn't bear to ask. Instead, she sat, frozen and unmoving, her hands clasped tightly in her lap. Outside beyond the broad windows of the tower, planes were beginning to take off in regular succession, and others were landing. There was continual chatter with their pilots over the radios. But when the one call signal she was waiting for finally came again, it brought nothing.

"Tower, Rescue one-four-six, come in."

"Roger, Rescue one-four-six, Tower here."

"Still nothing, Tower. Confirm coordinates."

They did so, then Dieter added, "Frank, how's your fuel looking?"

"We've got a couple more hours. Look, I'm just not getting this. There is nothing down there. I mean nothing. If a moose has been through here in the last couple of weeks, he didn't leave any trace. I've got a feeling we're just not looking in the right area."

"We were in contact, Frank. We got Shane's position not two minutes before he hit."

Hit. No more pretense, Brenna thought. No more "went down." Just plain "hit."

"We got what he thought was his position. But if it was, then where the hell is he? Where's anything?"

"The snow—"

"Snow, no snow, we'd see something. Anything on the search radio?"

"We had a burst an hour or so ago but it didn't go anywhere."

"How's the window looking?"

Dieter turned to Carl. "What's that new front doing?"

"Speeded up again. Forget thirty-six hours. We're definitely not looking at more than twenty-four."

When Dieter relayed this to Frank, the pilot said, "Then we damn well better make them count. This isn't working. Get out his flight plan and figure out exactly when he started icing. If we can nail down what the winds were doing, we might be able to get a handle on where he really ended up, not where his instruments were telling him he was."

"Roger that. We'll stay on station as long as the fuel holds out, then we're coming in. Let's see if we can get some new search data for a second try."

Dieter agreed. He handed the radio back to Carl and turned to the waiting men. "You heard what he said. It's all we've got now. Let's get on it."

They didn't know where Shane was. As Brenna watched the men move into the meeting room next to the tower to begin work, the full realization of what that meant sank in. From the beginning, the entire rescue effort had rested on the belief that they knew where Shane was when he lost control of his plane.

But they didn't. The plain fact was that they had no idea.

And without any, they had no way of knowing where to look.

A wave of dizziness washed over Brenna. She moaned softly.

A moment later—or more, she couldn't be sure— she felt a wet cloth gently touching her face and opened her eyes. Carol was staring at her. Softly, she asked, "Better?"

"I guess so. What happened?"

"You weren't looking so good. Look, I think we should get out of here for a while. Take a little walk, maybe get something besides this awful coffee to drink."

"I don't think—"

"I do." Firmly, Carol said, "Nothing's going to happen right now, honey. You know that. Those guys are going to do their job and I'm going to take care of you, so come on."

Brenna went. She was too strung out to argue and besides, Carol was right. If she sat around much longer, she was going to break.

They walked out into the main terminal. It was busier than before. With the airport open again, people were coming and going at a steady clip. Brenna looked at them with a feeling akin to wonder. All these people going about their ordinary lives seemed like part of another world, one she could see but couldn't touch, and certainly couldn't be part of. It was as though a plate glass wall had slammed down between her and the reality she had taken for granted.

It was still there all right. It just didn't have anything to do with her anymore.

Her reality, the only one that counted, was up there in the room next to the control tower where grimly intent men were trying desperately to figure out where in the vast Alaskan wilderness one small plane had fallen from the sky.

Chapter 14

They went to a bar. Brenna wasn't a drinker but just then she wanted a dark, quiet place to hide. The bar fit. They found a booth toward the back and settled in. A waitress came over, took their order, brought it promptly and disappeared. Perfect.

Brenna took a sip of her drink, put it down and looked at Carol. Her friend was exhausted. She had dark circles under her eyes. Her lower lip looked as though she'd been chewing on it. When she leaned her head back against the booth for a moment, Brenna thought she might have drifted off.

But with a visible effort, Carol pulled herself upright again. She gave herself a little shake and smiled apologetically. "Sorry."

"Don't be. You've got a perfect right to be worn out."

"Yeah, well, I'm not going through what you are.

I mean, I like Shane and all, but it isn't the same. I keep thinking how I'd feel if it had been Bob on that flight—'' She broke off abruptly. "Oh, honey, I'm sorry, that was awful to say."

"No it wasn't, it was just honest. It's okay, really. You know, Bob says he thinks it all came down to just plain bad luck. It's so hard for me to accept that but it could be true."

"It's so unfair. A person's life shouldn't depend on luck. Especially not a person like Shane. I mean, he worked so hard, didn't leave anything to chance, took responsibility, did all the things people are supposed to do. And then to think—"

"Sometimes you can do everything right and die anyway."

"That sounds like a quote."

"It is. A friend of my father's said it at his funeral. There was some talk after Dad was shot—why did he go into the alley, why didn't he wait for backup, that kind of thing. Anyway, the investigation turned up that there was a back exit to the alley. The guy Dad was chasing would just have gone out the other end and disappeared. He'd already shot two other people. There was no reason to think he was done. Dad weighed all that and went after him. Alone."

"I never knew this," Carol said softly. "I mean, I heard your father was killed in the line of duty but I never knew exactly what happened."

"That was it. Like his friend said, you can look at every aspect of a situation, make a strictly professional judgment, do everything right and end up dead anyway. It's just luck."

"We don't know that Shane's dead," Carol reminded her gently.

"No, but we both know that if he isn't and they don't find him soon, he will be. That new storm that's moving in basically guarantees it."

"People have survived for a long time out there, weeks even."

"If they're uninjured. Presuming for the moment that he's actually alive, what do you think the chances are that he came through such a crash uninjured?"

"Not real great," Carol admitted. "But we have to hope."

Brenna took another sip of her drink, put it down again. She really didn't want it. "I know, and I'm trying. It's just so hard. I wish—"

"Wish what?"

"Nothing. There's no point wishing. What's done is done."

"What's done? What do you mean?"

Brenna hesitated. Slowly, she said, "Shane and I had a fight, the night before he left, a bad one."

"Oh, honey—" Carol reached out a hand and covered hers.

"I really don't want to talk about it. Please understand, there's no way I can ever thank you enough for being here and doing so much. But this…this just goes too deep."

"It's okay," Carol said at once. "You don't have to talk about it. Look, I'm going to the ladies' room and on the way back, I'll see about getting us some food. Okay?"

Brenna nodded. She realized Carol was trying to

HOW TO VALIDATE YOUR
EDITOR'S FREE GIFT "THANK YOU"

1. Peel off gift seal from front cover. Place it in space provided at right. This automatically entitles you to receive four free books and a free Surprise Gift.

2. Send back this card and you'll get brand-new Silhouette Intimate Moments® novels. These books have a cover price of $3.99 each, but they are yours to keep absolutely free.

3. There's no catch. You're under no obligation to buy anything. We charge nothing — ZERO — for your first shipment. And you don't have to make any minimum number of purchases — not even one!

4. The fact is thousands of readers enjoy receiving books by mail from the Silhouette Reader Service™ months before they're available in stores. They like the convenience of home delivery and they love our discount prices!

5. We hope that after receiving your free books you'll want to remain a subscriber. But the choice is yours — to continue or cancel, anytime at all! So why not take us up on our invitation, with no risk of any kind. You'll be glad you did!

6. Don't forget to detach your FREE BOOKMARK. And remember...just for validating your Editor's Free Gift Offer, we'll send you FIVE MORE gifts, *ABSOLUTELY FREE!*

THIS SURPRISE MYSTERY GIFT CAN BE YOURS <u>FREE</u> AS ADDED THANKS FOR GIVING OUR READER SERVICE A TRY!

give her some time alone and she was deeply grateful for it. Somewhere along the line she must have done something right to have such a good friend.

When Carol had gone, Brenna sat for a time staring sightlessly at the far wall of the booth. Around her, the sounds of the bar were distant and muted. Almost without her being aware of it, her thoughts slipped away...

One month before

"Dr. O'Hare? Excuse me, Dr. O'Hare?"

Startled, Brenna looked up. She'd been so lost in her thoughts that she hadn't heard anyone come into the lab. A slender girl who appeared to be about fourteen years old was peering at her from behind very large glasses. "Are you Dr. O'Hare?"

"Yes, that's me. What can I do for you?"

The girl smiled, held out her hand, grasped Brenna's and pumped it vigorously. "Nice to meet you. I'm Trudi Blakely." When Brenna continued to look blank, she added, "The new research associate."

"Oh, yes, of course, Ms. Blakely." Not fourteen then, more like twenty-one but she looked so incredibly young... Or was it merely that she, Brenna, was a tad older?

"I was due in today," Ms. Blakely said. "We talked on the phone last week."

"Yes, of course we did. I'm sorry to be so preoccupied, it's just that I was—" lost in lustful thoughts about this incredible man I've been seeing. No, that wouldn't do at all.

"—tabulating data. That's it, I was tabulating data for the project. We're studying—"

"I know all about it. I've been reading your stuff for years, since I was in high school. I was so thrilled when I found out I'd be working with you."

"High school?" Brenna repeated numbly. She was twenty-eight years old, for heaven's sake. How could this kid have been reading her for *years*. But she could and she had and like it or not, Brenna had to admit it. In two more years, she'd be looking at thirty—a terrific age, definitely to be enjoyed—but still thirty. No wonder she'd been thinking about the future lately.

"Excuse me?" Trudi was saying something but Brenna had missed it.

"I just said I think I'm going to really like it here. Just now, when I was coming in, I saw the most incredibly hunky guy outside. I mean, I heard about Alaskan men before I came up here but I didn't really believe it. If he's anything to go by, it was all true. You wouldn't happen to know if he works here, would you?"

"What did he look like?" Brenna asked hurriedly. It was ten minutes to five. Shane had this thing about being on time, never late but not early, either.

"Six-four, shoulders out to here, this incredible golden hair like a mane and—"

"Listen, you know what? I think probably the best thing you could do right now is go over to wherever you're staying and get settled in. You've had a long trip, you're probably tired and—"

"I slept on the plane. Besides, traveling never bothers me."

Of course it didn't. She was too damn young to be bothered by anything.

"That's great, wonderful. Here, take this." She dumped a ream of printouts into Trudi's waiting arms.

"What is it?"

"Data from the sampling station in Prudhoe Bay. Look it over, do a correlation of water temperature and turbidity over the last six months, and get back to me on it tomorrow. Thanks, I really appreciate it."

Before Trudi could blink, Brenna was out the door. Not for nothing was she going to leave incredibly hunky Shane standing around outside for the likes of Ms. Blakely to salivate over.

"Hi," she said, just a little breathlessly when she skidded to a halt in front of him.

He smiled quizzically. "I'm early."

"That's okay. I'm ready. Let's go." She took his arm and steered him toward the curb where he'd parked. She'd left her own car at home, catching a lift with Carol. The always having two cars thing had gotten silly now that they were staying overnight at each other's places.

"How was work today?" he asked as he opened the passenger side door for her.

"Great. I got a new research assistant. Her name's Trudi and she thinks you're to die for."

Shane shut the door, went round the other side, got in behind the wheel, shut his door and said matter-of-factly, "I don't know any Trudi."

"And we're going to keep it that way."

He chuckled.

They went out to dinner at a small Japanese restaurant where they gorged themselves on sushi. When they came out, a light snow was falling. They ran back to the car. By the time they reached Brenna's house, the weather had worsened.

"Looks like we're finally getting some winter," Shane said as he helped her out.

"About time. There's still talk of a drought this spring."

"Do you get any vacation then?"

"Classes are off for a week. Why?"

"I was thinking maybe you'd like to go south, find a beach to lie on."

Take a vacation together? If anyone had told Brenna a month before that she'd be considering such a thing, she would have laughed. But her relationship with Shane had progressed—swiftly. Yes, that was a good way to put it. Swiftly. It sounded so much better than impulsively...or impetuously...or imprudently.

"Uh-oh," Shane said. "I can see the wheels going around."

She unlocked the front door and opened it. "Did you ever notice how many words there are that start with *I-M* and suggest a certain absence of reason?"

"Yeah, but then there are all those other *I-M* words, suggesting that something is irresistible—*implacable, imperious, imposing.*" He followed her inside, shutting the door behind them.

"You know the first time I met you, I thought it was really unfair that nature would give a man who looks like you a brain." At the glance he shot her, she relented—sort of. "Maybe unfair was the wrong word. Unnecessary."

"Are you telling me I'm just a pretty face as far as you're concerned?"

"Pretty face, great butt, a few other things—"

Shane growled and reached for her. She laughed and darted away, though not too far. He caught her by the stairs. They tussled playfully—and briefly. As always, she was struck by how very careful he was, keeping his strength in strict check. Even in the throes of passion, he never failed to do that.

She stopped suddenly, close against him, and touched her mouth to his. At the look in her eyes, he said, "What?"

"Nothing, I was just thinking...you really are a very special man."

"You're a very special woman. I know we haven't been together all that long but there are times when I think I've known you forever."

Brenna nodded. She understood exactly what he meant. There was a communion between them that she had never experienced before, and hadn't ever imagined was possible. In some fundamental way, he seemed like a missing piece of herself, found at last.

"You have an early flight," she reminded him and took his hand. They climbed the stairs to the bedroom together.

Chapter 15

Sunday

What was that? Through the fog of pain and fever, Shane thought he heard something. It was very distant and he couldn't be sure, but in the stillness any sound traveled far. He struggled to sit up, listening intently.

Nothing. All the same, he wasn't willing to write it off to imagination. It had been light long enough for the rescue choppers to be in the area. He had to make sure they saw him.

Crawling out of the survival tent, he squeezed his eyes shut against the sudden light. Instantly, his head throbbed. He ignored it, reached in the pack, and found a flare. Ideally, they should be used in darkness but he couldn't afford to be picky.

Unlike the radio, there wasn't a whole lot that

could happen to a flare, short of going off, that could damage it. He got one lit and watched with satisfaction as it soared into the sky. Several hundred feet up, it exploded, releasing a streaming contrail of red gas. Any pilot anywhere nearby ought to spot it.

He waited, hoping that any second he'd hear the sound of an approaching chopper. Nothing happened. After fifteen minutes or so, he forced himself to acknowledge that it wasn't going to happen. Not yet anyway. Give them a little more time. They'd find him.

With his strength going fast, he crawled back into the tent and huddled under the blankets. Waves of heat and cold swept him alternately. His leg was pure, burning agony. Another thing he had to face—the antibiotic definitely wasn't working.

Grimly, he wondered how much time that meant he had. He swallowed a couple more of the analgesics and lay back down. If he got out of this—no, when he got out of this—he was going to be damn sure that survival packs carried a variety of antibiotics including whatever happened to be newest. At the rate bacteria were wising up, it was all-out war.

When he got back... On that thought, he drifted off again, as though down a long, slowly moving current that was carrying him away from shore.

Shores had beaches. He was looking forward to getting somewhere warm with Brenna, somewhere with palm trees, tropical breezes and slow dancing under the moon. He could just see her, wearing something gauzy, light and graceful in his arms, laughing.

She had a real sense of humor, not the brittle, phony kind but the genuine article.

He laughed softly. What was it she'd said? Oh, yeah, that pretty face, great butt remark. Okay, so he was flattered, sue him. But he hadn't done anything to come by his looks and sometimes they embarrassed him. Not that he'd ever admitted that to anyone, but it was true all the same. There had been times when he was with a woman when he wondered if she had any idea, much less cared, that he had an actual mind—and a heart.

Maybe it wasn't exactly macho to care, but it was how he felt. And so did Brenna. She could actually tease him about how he looked at the same time she recognized there was somebody real on the inside.

He thought he knew why that was. She was a very lovely woman, the kind men would normally have been panting after. But she had a tendency to downplay her looks, except for that first date and the dress she'd worn.

Floating, no longer really sure where he was or particularly caring, he smiled. That was some dress. But aside from that, she didn't make a big deal of herself. She also didn't hide the fact that she was smart. He suspected there were plenty of jerks who couldn't deal with that.

Their loss, his gain. He could see her being smart and funny and terrific to be with all her life, decades and decades into the future. The point was, he really wanted to see it. He wanted to be there with her, sharing it all.

His smile faded. There was a problem with that.

He couldn't quite remember what it was. Maybe that meant it didn't matter very much. He relaxed again, remembering.

One month earlier...

They'd gone out to the Japanese restaurant they liked. It was snowing when they got back to her place. Upstairs, in the bedroom, she moved away from him. As he watched, she began to undress, very matter-of-factly, as though she were completely alone.

He sat down on the bed, enjoying the sight. She took off her shoes first, hopping on one foot and then the other. The skirt she wore was a little tight, just enough to restrict her. Stretching, she eased her blouse out of the waistband and began undoing the buttons. When she finished, she left the blouse on, hanging open.

With a little sigh, as though she felt tired, she undid the skirt and slipped it off. Her long, slender legs were clad in black silk stockings held in place by garters attached to a sheer white silk teddy that was cut high on her hips and left much of her rounded buttocks bare. Strategically placed embroidery covered but did not conceal her nipples and the cleft between her thighs.

Slowly, she removed her blouse and laid it on a chair beside the skirt. In the same unhurried way, she raised one foot, balanced it on the seat of the chair and unfastened the first stocking. Shane watched as she peeled it down her leg and slid it off over her foot. The second followed.

His body was rock hard, his breathing strained, but he didn't move. She was so utterly natural in her movements, so exquisitely feminine and sensual, that he almost hated to have this end. But it had to, of course. He simply couldn't stand it much longer.

As she laid the second stocking aside, he rose, strode across the room and slid a commanding arm around her waist.

"Very nice," he murmured, feeling the heat of her body through the single layer of fragile silk. One tear and—

"I'm so glad you like it," she murmured.

"If I liked it any more—" He moved his lower body against her, his readiness obvious.

She made a sound that sounded very like a purr and turned in his arms. "Anyone ever tell you that you wear too many clothes?"

"Only a certain pushy broad."

"I'll assume that's me."

"That would be safe," Shane said. She was undoing the buttons of his shirt with the same dexterous skill she'd brought to the blouse. When she was done, she slid it off. Her breath, warm and soft, moved over his flesh. Her lips followed. A deep, pounding tremor raced through him.

"I'm not feeling safe," she said and undid his belt buckle. Her hand brushed against him, lingering.

"Good." His fingers closed around her wrists. Love play was one thing, this was pure torture. Zooplankton be damned, the woman had missed her calling.

Or she'd just recently discovered it.

He rather liked that thought. It might even be true. For all her boldness, there was a lingering innocence about Dr. Brenna O'Hare that was nothing short of intoxicating.

Which was all very well and good, but there were limits to his patience and he had reached them.

Swiftly, he lifted her and carried her over to the bed. His mouth teased her nipples through the embroidered silk as his hand slid between her legs to unsnap the teddy. Baring her to the waist, he spread her thighs. She moaned softly, hands clinging to him.

He released his hardness but didn't bother to finish undressing. Turning her so that she lay facedown beneath him, he raised her hips and entered her in a single long, deep thrust. As ready as he was, as filled with need, she tightened around him, drawing him even farther into her.

He closed his eyes against the undulating waves of pleasure and thrust again. They moved together, again and again, driving each other higher and higher, until release seized them both suddenly.

Gasping, Shane fell onto the bed, drawing her with him. He held her tenderly, stroking her back, as the world slowly returned around them. When it had at last, Brenna raised herself on an elbow, gave him a purely lascivious smile and asked, "Does sushi usually do this to you?"

"Planning to corner the market on toro?"

"Something like that. You're still overdressed."

"If I could move, I'd fix that."

She raised an eyebrow. "Oh, well, if you're too tired…"

He gave her a baleful look. "You like to live dangerously, don't you?"

"What did I say? You worked all day, went out to dinner, it's only natural you're tired. After all, you're not eighteen anymore and—"

"I've got news for you, lady. I couldn't have handled you when I was eighteen."

"And you can now?"

"Let's just say I've got a damn sight better chance. Come here."

She ignored him and slid off the bed. The sight of her, still clad only in the silky teddy bunched around her waist, made him realize that he really wasn't tired at all.

"I think I'll just get into something more comfortable," she said and stepped out of the teddy.

Shane grinned. Definitely not tired. He folded his arms behind his head. "What did you have in mind?"

"You'll see."

She walked over to the dressing table, every movement graceful and utterly feminine. Selecting a cut crystal bottle, she removed the stopper and took a sniff. "My favorite perfume. It's a blend of hyacinth, rose and sandalwood."

"Sounds great."

"Of course, it has to be used very sparingly. It has certain...potent effects."

"Does it?" His voice was just a touch rough around the edges.

She nodded. Her eyes danced with humor but she tried very hard to look serious. "For instance, if I place just a little here—'' She touched the stopper to the cleft between her breasts. "It's very pleasant."

"I can see how it would be."

"And if I add a little more here—" Carefully, she cupped each breast in her hand and applied just a bit of the perfume beneath the rounded fullness. "That's even better."

"Hmmm."

"And if I—" She parted her legs and touched the crystal stopper to the inside of her thighs.

"Come back here."

"But I'm not done yet."

"Yes, you are." He stepped off the bed, shed the rest of his clothes in one swift motion and crossed the room to her. The crystal perfume bottle did make it back onto the dresser but just barely.

Chapter 16

Sunday

Brenna surprised herself. She was actually able to eat something. The bar had a chicken soup nobody's mother would have been ashamed to call her own. She passed up the sandwiches Carol had also ordered but did put her drink aside and had a glass of milk instead. By the time they left, she was feeling better.

That faded as soon as they returned to the control tower. "The choppers have to return," Bob said quietly. "They're almost out of fuel."

Brenna nodded. She'd known this was coming. "Any luck figuring out where he really is?"

"The guys are still working. There are so many variables—"

From the room where the men were gathered, she

heard a muted curse. When she glanced through the door, the scene was stark and telling. Someone had brought in a couple of computers on carts. Their screens glowed. Rows of figures marched across them. As she watched, one of the men switched windows, bringing up a map marked with wind currents. He said something to another and shook his head.

"It's tough," Bob said.

Quietly, Brenna replied. "It looks impossible."

"Given enough time…"

"But there isn't, is there? Not with that new front closing in. Unless he can get the radio to work—" She looked at Bob.

He shook his head. "There hasn't been anything."

She felt very cold. The soup that had tasted so good a short while ago lay like lead in her stomach. "I think I'll just get a drink of water," she said and slipped away.

In the small ladies' room, she splashed her face and dried it with a rough paper towel. Her hair looked as though she'd slept in it. The thought seemed funny somehow. She started to smile but grimaced instead and put her head down.

The tears that had threatened for so long came finally. When they were done, she washed her face again, then leaned against the wall beside the sink. She was so tired but sleep seemed something barely remembered. She could hardly recall what it felt like to lie down in bed, stretch out all warm and comfortable and let herself drift off, knowing that Shane was there beside her and would be all through the night—

One month earlier

She was getting so very used to his being there. Fighting to stay awake just a few minutes longer, Brenna gazed at Shane lying on his side facing her. He was already asleep but then who could blame the man? He'd definitely earned it.

The sense of wonder she felt so often with him was no less powerful for being familiar. He astounded her not in the least because of the way he made her astound herself. Never in her wildest imaginings would she have believed she could behave as she did with him. Yet with him, all things seemed possible, even inevitable.

He made her feel so safe. Surely, that was an illusion? Life didn't offer any safety. She had watched her mother learn that lesson and never forgot it herself. It was a whole lot better to care about zooplankton than about any particular human being.

But she'd gone and done it anyway. Like it or not, she cared for Shane a great deal. After only a month, she could scarcely imagine life without him.

With a small sigh, she pulled the covers up more securely over them both. The snow was continuing. It was likely Shane's flight would be delayed. They'd have more time together in the morning.

On that thought, she drifted into sleep. But there she found not rest but uneasy dreams. She was standing in a room she recognized but could not put a name to. People were coming and going, talking gravely among themselves. No one seemed to see her. It was as though she had become invisible.

As she wandered through the room, the crowd parted suddenly and she found herself staring at a coffin set on a table. A woman sat on a chair beside it, her face consumed by grief. She looked up and alone among all the people, saw Brenna. Her mouth moved but no words could be heard. She raised a hand, gesturing Brenna nearer.

She did not want to go but found herself moving forward. Only then did she realize that the woman was her mother and she was pulling her toward the coffin. Brenna hung back, trying with all her strength, but the dream overpowered her. The coffin was open. Terrified, choking on tears, she was forced to look at the face of the man lying there so still and unmoving....

"Nooo!"

She woke screaming and sat bolt upright in bed. Her heart hammered against her ribs. She was shaking all over.

"*Brenna...*" Instantly, Shane's arms were around her. He clasped her tightly as she clung to him, her head buried against his chest. Murmuring soothing words, he stroked her hair until finally she began to calm.

When she had, he set her aside a little so that he could look at her. His eyes were filled with concern. "That must have been some dream."

At the mere mention of it, she stiffened. "Nightmare...I don't usually have them." She took a deep breath, fighting for control. The shadow of terror still lay heavily upon her. "I'm sorry."

"You don't have to apologize, it's okay." He

touched the back of his hand lightly to her cheek in a gesture that was infinitely tender. "Feeling better?"

She managed a weak smile. "A little."

"How about a drink of water?"

"No," she said quickly, realizing that he would leave the bed to get it for her. She couldn't bear him being gone just then.

"All right." He lay back down, drawing her with him. She lay in the protective circle of his arms, her head on his broad shoulder, as her heartbeat slowly returned to normal.

"You should go back to sleep," she said softly. "The weather might still clear and you'll have to fly."

He settled the covers around her, almost as though she were a child in need of tucking in. "Don't worry about it. Do you have nightmares like that very often?"

"No, especially not like that." She laughed shakily. "It was a humdinger."

"So I gathered. Sometimes it can help to talk about it."

Brenna hesitated. The dream really had left her with a residue of stark dread. She hated to even think about it, much less give it voice. But on the other hand, she and Shane were certainly close enough now that he deserved some explanation.

"I'm not really sure, it's starting to fade a little, but I think it had to do with when my father was killed."

He turned slightly so that he was looking at her.

"You mentioned that once but we never really talked about it. What happened?"

Briefly, Brenna told him. She concluded, "My mother told me much later that being a policeman's wife, she'd lived with the fear of my father dying every day for so many years that it had become second nature. But when the knock finally came at the door, she realized that she was still totally unprepared to deal with it."

"Did she tell you this when you were dating the guy who was a cop?"

"Yes, that's when we finally talked about it. We never had before but I think at that point she felt there were certain things she needed to say, or at least give me an opportunity to ask."

"And it was then that you decided not to marry him?"

"I just couldn't see living the way she had. She told me that there were times when they'd be having dinner together and the phone would ring. He'd have to go out and she'd sit there wondering if he was going to come back. She didn't say it like I should feel sorry for her. She was just being honest."

"You said that if you'd loved the guy, you would have been able to get past it."

Brenna nodded. "Big if. I just don't think it's in me to fall in love with a man whose life involves that kind of danger."

Shane was quiet for several moments. Finally, he said, "There are all kinds of danger."

"Oh, I know that. Heck, some people think flying

is dangerous.'' She looked at him teasingly. ''But I hear you're a pretty good pilot, so—''

''Pretty good?''

''Well, yeah, but with a great—''

''Enough, woman.'' He moved suddenly, putting her under him. His big hands cupped her face. In the shadows of light reflecting off the new-fallen snow, his features looked hard and unrelenting, but his touch was gentle.

''I think I'd better give you something else to think about,'' he said.

And did.

Sunday

There was no doubt about it, Shane was the ultimate distraction. With him, she forgot about everything else—the world beyond the two of them, the lessons of the past, everything.

She had even managed to forget about the nightmare—until now. It must be true what the brain researchers said—memories burrowed deep but they didn't disappear. They could pop up any time, without any warning.

Standing there in the bathroom, her chest so tight that she could hardly breathe, she remembered every detail of that nightmare. Including the one detail she had never let herself think about until that very moment.

It hadn't been her father lying there in the coffin.

It had been Shane.

Bile rose in the back of her throat. She leaned over

the sink, turned the tap on, and forced herself to drink a small amount of water. It helped, although not much.

Wetting a towel, she pressed it to her eyes until colored lights danced behind them. Her mind was playing tricks on her. She had twisted the dream to reflect her fears in the present.

But try though she did to convince herself of that, the image of Shane lying there, his head resting on a white satin pillow, his features cold and still, was burned into her brain. She couldn't deny or forget it.

A month ago, before everything went wrong, some deeply buried part of her had already sensed what might happen.

Or what would happen?

Which was it? Had she somehow glimpsed the future?

Instantly, she rejected that. She had never had anything remotely resembling an extrasensory experience in her life and she didn't believe she was having one now. At most, the nightmare simply reflected her own most deeply rooted fears. She'd realized that she was falling in love with Shane and worried about where that would lead. There was nothing more to it.

The fact that within a handful of days, she might be standing in front of a coffin, saying farewell to Shane forever, was only a coincidence. A horrible, terrifying one, to be sure, but nothing more.

She had not seen the future.

"I didn't," she whispered fiercely, desperate to convince herself. And as she did, something feather-light brushed her mind. It was so faint that she might easily have missed it. Holding herself absolutely still, afraid to think or move, she felt it again.

A long, slow breath filled her lungs. And with it a conviction grew within her, a strange, elusive and yet powerful sense that Shane really was alive. For the merest fragment of an instant, it was as though he were standing right there beside her.

He was alive. She felt that to the depths of her very soul. The experience was so intense that she shook with the very force of it. By comparison, the nightmare seemed like nothing more than an annoyance.

He was alive. She knew it as surely as if he had just reached out and touched her.

Without hesitation, Brenna yanked open the door to the ladies room and walked swiftly back to the control tower. Bob was the first person she encountered.

"They can't give up," she said emphatically. "Tell them that. They've got to figure out where he is."

"Honey, they are, they're doing everything they—"

"No, I mean it. They've got to. Shane's alive."

Bob stared at her. There was no doubt what he was thinking. "We all want that to be true—" he began gently.

"I'm not crazy," Brenna said. All her weariness was gone. "It's not grief talking, or worry, or anything like that. He's alive. I don't know how I know, but I do."

"You may be right," Bob said cautiously, "and we're all going on the assumption that you are but—"

He never got to finish the sentence. Carl jumped

suddenly in his seat and clamped his hands to the headphones. Over the murmur of controllers guiding planes in and out, his voice rang sharp and clear.

"I've got something."

Chapter 17

Sunday

It was Brenna who woke him. He'd been dreaming of her again and it had been so real that he thought she was really there. That was enough to drag him out of feverish sleep, only to discover that he was still very much alone.

Yet the impression of her was so strong that Shane couldn't shake it. For just an instant, he could have sworn that she was right there with him.

He shook his head, angry at his own flights of fancy. The fever must be doing strange things to his brain. But it didn't prevent him from realizing that he had drifted off again just when he most needed to be alert.

A glance at his watch made him curse. He'd been

out for more than an hour. Any search choppers in the area could have come and gone without his ever knowing.

Moreover, it would start to get dark soon. He couldn't just lie there and do nothing. Picking up the radio again, he stared at it. Why wouldn't the damn thing work?

The fever made it hard to concentrate but he forced himself, going very slowly, running down the mental checklist of everything he'd ever learned about radios. The exercise reminded him of the story he'd heard— more than once—about the test pilot who runs into trouble. He radios in that he's "tried A and tried B and tried C, so what do I do now?" And the reply comes back: "Shut up and die like an aviator."

He'd tried A and all the rest. Hell, he'd gone all the way to Z and still the damn thing put out nothing but static. He flicked the switch again, more by force of habit at this point, and suddenly stiffened. There was static, all right, but not as much as before.

Slowly, he hit the transmit button and raised the radio closer to his mouth. "Anchorage Tower, Anchorage Tower, this is Aleut niner-four-niner. Pilot down. Repeat, pilot down. Come in, Tower."

Nothing.

He tried it again. The static was worsening. Whatever was causing it—and he was convinced now that it was an atmospheric disturbance—wasn't giving up. But just when he thought he might have to, he heard something.

"...tower...break..recep...poor..."

Elation roared through him. They had him, or at

least they would if he could just stay on the air long enough.

"Anchorage Tower, roger that, this is Aleut niner-four-niner, pilot down. Say search position, repeat say search position."

"...come in..."

They hadn't heard him. His grip tightened on the radio. Holding his voice steady, he said, "Anchorage Tower, this is Aleut niner-four-niner, I am down and injured. No search choppers sighted this location. Say position, repeat say position."

Nothing. The static intensified, wiping out anything that might have been behind it.

Long minutes passed before Shane forced himself to accept that. His face was grim as he switched the radio off. It was vital that he conserve the batteries. Eventually, the weather would change, the interference would lessen. He would try again.

Assuming, of course, that he was in any condition to do so.

"I've got something," Carl shouted.

Silence fell in the control tower. No one moved. Brenna could have sworn no one was even breathing.

Carl switched the radio to the loudspeaker. There was a burst of static and then—

"...four...pilot...repeat..."

The voice was faint and distant, also masked by the static, but it was unmistakably a man's.

John Dieter took up the mike. He spoke slowly and calmly.

"This is Anchorage Tower, you're breaking up, reception is poor, say again."

The only response was static.

Dieter waited several moments, then tried again. "This is Anchorage Tower. We are not receiving you clearly. Send again. Repeat, send again. Come in..."

Nothing.

Brenna realized she had clenched her fists so tightly that her nails were digging into the palms of her hands. Slowly, she released them.

No one moved. Finally, Dieter put the mike down. Quietly, he said, "If I ever find out somebody was broadcasting on this frequency without clearance, I will personally shove the son of a bitch out over the Aleutians."

"It could have been him," Bob said.

The men who had come in from the workroom glanced at each other. One or two nodded.

"It could have been," Dieter agreed. He turned to Carl. "You got everything on tape?"

"Absolutely."

"Okay. I want it washed and rewashed. If there's anything under there, you bring it up. Got that?"

"Got it," Carl murmured. He turned back to his workstation with fierce concentration.

"What does he mean?" Brenna asked.

"Static doesn't destroy transmissions," Bob explained. "It just covers them up. Under all the junk there may be an actual message. Carl has to try to find it."

"How?"

"By eliminating everything else. Of course, the

problem lies in figuring out what's garbage and what isn't.''

"And that takes time..." She could fill in the rest for herself. Time that they didn't have.

"Carl's very good. He could get lucky. We all could."

Luck again. She was learning to hate it.

"The choppers will be landing in fifteen minutes," Bob said. "They'll refuel and take off again immediately. By the time they reach the search area, we should have something."

"And we'll be almost out of light."

"That's true," he agreed, "but if we can raise Shane and he knows when to set off his flares, they'll be seen for miles. Night's actually better for that."

"As long as it stays clear."

"As long as."

"I'm going for a walk," Brenna said. She turned on her heel and walked out of the control room. It was all she could do not to run.

Shane was alive. She knew it. That had been him on the radio but she'd known he was alive before then in a way she didn't understand but didn't question either.

However, the knowing gave her no comfort. He was alive now. Would he be in the morning?

For a few minutes, she wandered aimlessly through the terminal. A sign caught her eye. She hesitated, then walked toward it.

A covered passageway led to a small, modern building set a little apart from the main terminal. Its

unadorned simplicity gave it a kind of elegance. The bronze plaque on the door read:
Ecumenical Chapel—All Are Welcome.

Brenna eased the door open and stepped inside. Beyond it were several rows of chairs facing a slightly raised dais on which a display of fresh spring flowers was arranged in a pottery vase. On the wall behind, an abstract stained glass window drew the eye upward.

True to its name, the chapel offered no symbols of any particular religion. But it still provided exactly the peace and solitude she most desperately needed.

Taking a chair toward the front, she sat down. For a few minutes, the chaos of her thoughts was a clamor in her mind. But eventually they stilled. She felt quiet deep within herself and reached for it. Only to find that, even there, memories waited.

Two weeks earlier...

"Want to go for a ride?" Shane asked.

Brenna looked up from the toast she'd been buttering and shrugged. "Sure, why not?"

It was a Sunday. Neither of them had to be anywhere or do anything in particular, and it looked as though they were in for some good weather. "Where did you have in mind?" she asked as she refilled his coffee cup.

He grinned. "You'll see."

Her first clue came when they took the airport exit. Shane was behind the wheel. He shot her a teasing look. "Ever hear of a busman's holiday?"

"Don't tell me. When you aren't working, you love watching the planes take off and land."

"Hell, no. I haven't done that since I was a kid and I hated it then. All I could think of was how long it would be before I could get behind the controls."

"Oh..." It was beginning to dawn on her what he'd actually meant by a ride.

On a sudden thought, he asked, "Hey, you like to fly, don't you?"

"It's okay."

"Okay?" They pulled into a parking spot in front of the building that housed Air Aleut. Shane went around to open the door for her. He always did that despite the fact that she always let herself out first. It was a little game they both enjoyed.

"You think flying is just okay?" he asked as they walked into the building.

"Well, okay's good, isn't it?"

"No, it's okay." He flicked on a couple of lights and went over to check the latest weather reports. "Have you flown much?"

"About the usual, I guess. Vacations here and there, research trips, you know."

"And you understand the basic principles."

Brenna hesitated. She was a scientist, for heaven's sake. She was supposed to know stuff. "You mean why the plane flies?"

"Right, you understand all that."

"Well...it flies because it has engines. They make it fly."

He put the weather reports down and stared at her. "My car has an engine. It doesn't fly."

"That's a different kind of engine. Besides—" She was in bad shape already so she figured she might as well make it worse. "I'm a girl. I don't need to know things like that."

He laughed, reminding her yet again of exactly why she was so attracted to him. No, besides *that*. He knew when she was kidding. Too many people she'd met didn't.

"Very funny," Shane said. "You'd like flying more if you understood how it works."

"Why don't we stay right here and you can explain it to me?" Seeing what he thought of that, she tried another tack. "Or we could get one of those flight simulator programs and pretend we're in air-to-air combat over Nazi Germany. Cool, huh?"

"Terrific, but I've got a sweet little two-seater out there I've been neglecting lately and she needs some attention. Come on."

As he headed for the door, Brenna followed, but hesitantly. She didn't want to look like a total dweeb but on the other hand, flying was definitely not her favorite thing to do.

"When you say attention," she said, "you don't mean the mechanical kind?"

"Don't I? Best way to figure out what's wrong with a plane is to take it up and see what doesn't work."

Brenna made a strangled noise.

Shane laughed. "I'm sorry," he said, looking not remotely apologetic. "It's just that you're so much fun to tease. No, the plane is in perfect condition but she's the first one I ever actually owned and I've got a soft spot for her.''

"Oh, great, sounds like a rival."

"So here's your chance to size her up. Besides, it's a perfect day for flying. We'll be able to see for miles."

She mustered a smile similar to the one she'd given the dentist. They walked out onto the tarmac. A small plane was sitting there. The words *Air Aleut* were painted on its tail. Brenna cast it a baleful look. The plane wasn't more than fifteen feet long from end to end. Moreover, she could actually see all of it. As a general rule, she didn't fly in anything she could see. Planes should be approached through connecting passageways that led directly from the waiting area to the cabin with no unpleasant glimpses of wings and such like in between.

"Nice, huh?" Shane said, following her glance.

"It's great...for a small plane."

"That one's not small." At her startled glance, he smiled tolerantly, took her arm and led her around the other side of the plane. There, sitting where it had been completely blocked from view by the "small" aircraft, sat another plane. At least, she supposed it was a plane and not simply a large mechanical bird.

"That's what is generally considered to be a small plane," Shane said.

"My car is bigger." Incredibly, that was true.

"Not if you take the wing span into account," he told her cheerfully and opened the very small door that took up most of one very small side. "You first."

She had to crawl in. When she'd finally managed

to get into one of the two seats and wiggle herself into what felt like a remotely comfortable position, she said, "Do you actually fly this or just wear it?"

He laughed. "A little of both. Need any help with those belts?"

They were different from what she was used to. Besides the usual lap belt, there were two that came down over her shoulders.

"I've got them," she said after struggling for a moment. "Do I get a helmet, too?"

"I don't use one. Keeps me from feeling the wind in my hair." Quickly, he added, "Joke, just a joke. That's all. Joke."

"Lousy joke."

"Sorry. Now, settle back, you're going to love this."

Yeah, right. But she didn't say it. He was so enthusiastic and he wanted so much for her to share at least a tiny bit of his pleasure in flying. She couldn't bring herself to be any more discouraging than she already had been.

At least, she didn't think she could.

He started the engine. Wonderful, there was only one of them. It seemed to rev up very quickly. Within minutes, the whole cabin was vibrating.

With an encouraging smile in her direction, Shane pivoted the plane in a tight circle and headed out onto the runway. He said something into the radio, listened, said something more and flipped a few switches in front of him.

The whine of the engine was now so loud that any conversation was impossible. Not that Brenna had any particular desire to talk. It was all she could do to breathe. They were bouncing down the runway, gathering speed with every second. Just when she thought they were going to shake apart, the plane leapt into the air. She glanced out the very small window just in time to see the ground falling away at an alarming rate.

A few moments later, the pitch of the engine suddenly changed. It became quiet enough to at least hear what Shane was saying.

"See, nothing to it. A plane like this is made for the sky. It never really feels right on the ground."

"But it feels right now...?"

"Sure, perfect."

"It just sounded...different."

He shot her a gently chiding look. "It's supposed to. We've reached our flight speed so we're no longer accelerating. The engine isn't working as hard as it was during takeoff."

"That makes sense."

"The whole thing makes sense. The engine draws in a current of air and pushes it out behind us, creating the thrust that moves us forward. It's really so simple that it's surprising it took as long as it did to work out."

"The only thing actually keeping us in the air is the air? That's what you're saying?"

He nodded, pleased that she'd gotten it. "Great, isn't it? Of course, we're talking here about a propeller engine. Jet engines work differently. They not only take in air, but compress some of it and heat that to produce hot gas with a lot of additional thrust."

"You're overlooking something."

"What's that?"

"The sheer force of will of the passengers holding the plane up."

"Well, that's important, too."

Despite herself, Brenna had to admit that this was better than she'd expected. Now that they were airborne, she no longer felt as though her kidneys were being shaken to bits. The sky was a pure crystalline blue sparkling with sunlight. Below, the winter landscape looked austerely beautiful.

"Told you," Shane said. He'd been watching the change in her expression.

"Don't rub it in."

"Okay, pay attention now."

"Why?" she asked suspiciously. She'd already been suckered into flying in a plane that looked as though it had come out of a cereal box. What more did Shane have in mind?

"You have to know what the instruments are for before you take the controls."

"Before I—" He was nuts. Gorgeous, sexy, funny, wonderful, terrific—and nuts. "Oh, no, absolutely not. No way, no how. Forget it."

"You'll love it."

"No, I won't. Really, I won't. You can let me out here."

"This is the altimeter. It measures height above sea level in feet."

"No."

"This is the air speed indicator. It's calibrated in knots."

"No."

"And this is your attitude indicator. You want to keep this pretty much level."

"No."

"Put both hands on the control column like this and just relax."

Her hands gripped what looked like a steering wheel with the top cut off, but only because she needed to hold on to something.

"Under your feet are the rudder pedals. You won't be using those so move your feet back a little."

"I'm not using anything. I can't—"

"Switching control over to you."

And he did. She felt it the second it happened. Suddenly, there was power in her hands.

"Oh, my God!"

"Easy now. Just keep her nice and steady. Watch the attitude indicator. See that line there? That's the horizon. You want to stay level with that."

"You can't do this! I can't!"

"Sure you can. You are. Now, we want to make a slow turn to the right. It's not a whole lot different from making a turn in your car except you have to think in three dimensions. Stay at the same altitude, keep the nose level and just ease her in."

"Think of all the other poor innocent people who are in the sky right now. They don't deserve to die like this."

"It's Sunday morning, traffic's light. Actually, it's nonexistent. I checked. And you're doing fine."

Brenna shot him a quick glance, all she dared when

she was frantically watching the dials in front of her.
Incredibly, nothing terrible seemed to be happening.

"Okay, good, now level her off again."

"Like this?"

"Yep, just like that. You learn fast. Maybe I could
catch a little nap."

Brenna laughed. That amazed her. She adjusted her
hands on the column and relaxed ever so slightly.
Maybe she wasn't going to get them killed, after all.

"I guess I can see how someone could get to like
this," she admitted.

"Nothing beats it. Well, okay, maybe one thing
but—"

"Don't distract me. What's that dial for?"

"That? Shows how much fuel you've got. Do I
distract you?"

"And that?"

"Compass. A lot?"

"No, I think you're the most boring man I've ever
met. I alternate between wanting to wring your neck,
which by the way is top priority right now, and wanting to do a few other things it would be better not to
get into at the moment."

He grinned. "Just a few? I think you're underes-
timating yourself."

"If anybody had ever told me—"

"What?"

She hesitated. How could they possibly be having
this conversation while she was flying—flying!— a
plane. No doubt about it, he turned her life upside
down.

"Let's just say you weren't on my schedule."

"What was?"

"I don't know," she admitted. "More of the same, I guess. Work, life, the usual."

"That's how I felt. Then you showed up at Carol and Bob's wearing that blue dress and I had to reconsider."

"Oh, so it was the dress?" She made a show of exasperation.

"No, of course not, what do you take me for? It was what was *in* the dress."

"Not my sparkling personality?"

"Your what?"

"Or my blinding intellect?"

"Huh?"

"My rapierlike repartee?"

"Does that mean you talk nice?"

"It means it's lucky for you I'm terrified to let go of this thing."

"You have to admit that was some dress."

"I might even be persuaded to wear it again sometime."

He looked interested. "Oh, yeah? How?"

"You could start by telling me how much longer I'm going to be flying this thing."

"Not too much. Take her through a couple of loop-the-loops, do a death spiral or two, and we'll call it a day."

"All right."

"Whoa! I think maybe it's time we switched back."

So did Brenna but she didn't see any reason to admit it. "C'mon, just one loop-the-loop."

"Maybe next time."

She sat back as he took control and eased the plane into a leisurely descent. As they were landing, she thought with amazement of what she had done. Being with Shane was filled with all sorts of surprises. He challenged her to be more than she had ever been before.

But was she really equal to it? Or was all this simply more than she could bear?

Chapter 18

Sunday

Brenna raised her head slowly. She felt as though she had been very far away. For a moment, she had difficulty remembering where she was. Then her gaze settled on the stained-glass window at the far end of the chapel and a low sigh ran through her.

It was very quiet. No one had intruded on her solitude and she was glad of it. Beyond the chapel walls, she could hear the muted sounds of the airport but they might have been part of another world. Here there was only peace...and prayer.

Lost in contemplation, she didn't recognize the sound at first. Several moments passed before she realized that the chapel door had creaked open. Brenna glanced over her shoulder. Carol was there.

She came over to where Brenna was sitting. Her mouth quivered, as though she was laughing and crying all at the same time. Very simply, she said, "Carl did it."

Brenna had no memory of reaching the control room. She might have flown through the terminal for all she knew. When she rushed in, the men were all gathered around Carl's station. John Dieter saw her first and gestured her over.

He put a burly arm around her shoulders and said, "That's a hell of a guy you're hooked up with, honey. Listen to this." He pushed a button on the console. A tape began to run.

There was a burst of static and then, faint but unmistakable, Shane's voice: "Anchorage Tower, Anchorage Tower, this is Aleut niner-four-niner... down. Repeat, pilot down. Come...tower."

"It's still choppy," Dieter said, "but Carl did one bang-up job."

Brenna nodded, all her attention focused on the tape. She heard Dieter's voice, calm and slow: "This is Anchorage Tower, you're breaking up, reception is poor, say again."

And then Shane: "Anchorage...roger...Aleut niner-four-niner, pilot down...search position, repeat...position—"

And Dieter again: "This is Anchorage Tower. We are not receiving you clearly. Send again. Repeat, send again. Come in..."

"Anchorage Tower, this is Aleut niner-four-niner, I am down and injured. No choppers sighted this location. Say position, repeat say position."

"That's it," Dieter said. He switched the tape off and gave Carl a big grin. "When this is all over, I owe you a drink."

"I'll take it," Carl said. He looked utterly drained but elated at the same time.

Brenna might have felt the same but there was only one thought in her mind.

"He's injured."

Dieter nodded. "Yes, but he's conscious, he's able to talk and he's got at least some awareness of what's happening around him. He's also told us something we need to know."

"Which is?"

"That the odds are very high we've been looking in the wrong place."

"The choppers have finished refueling," Bob interjected. "They're ready to go."

"Get me Frank," Dieter said. When he had the senior rescue pilot on the radio, he told him what they'd been able to learn. "Shane's alive but injured. He hasn't seen any more sign of you guys than you've seen of him. We've got to work out a different search pattern."

"Anything on that possible course change?" Frank asked.

"We're still crunching the numbers but I hope to have something in another hour or so. We'll get it to you as soon as we can."

"Roger that. Out."

Brenna moved over to the plate glass windows overlooking the runway. She watched as one by one, the choppers took off.

"Okay," Dieter said. "Now let's see if there's any chance we can raise our boy." He picked up the radio. "Aleut niner-four-niner, this is Anchorage Tower. Come in."

Nothing. But Dieter refused to be discouraged. He repeated the call. This time, in amid the static, it seemed to Brenna that there was something else. She strained forward, listening.

Nothing.

"We could be in the clear at his end and not even know it," Carl said.

Dieter nodded. "Which is why we're going to keep at it. Somehow, we've got to raise him before Frank and the others get to wherever it is we're going to send them this time." All his frustration and concern were clear in his voice, but he looked perfectly calm as he handed the radio back to Carl. "Keep sending. Don't stop. Instruct him that the coordinates we have are believed to be wrong and we must have new ones. Also, give him the ETA of the rescue choppers in the general area of his last transmission and tell him they'll stay on post as long as they have fuel."

"Will do," Carl said.

"Let's hope he gets at least some of that."

"And if he doesn't?" Brenna asked quietly.

Dieter shook his head. "I don't have an answer for that."

"Aleut niner-four-niner," Carl was saying. "This is Anchorage Tower. Rescue is airborne but without co-ordinates. Say again, rescue is airborne—"

Carol was standing a little off to one side. Brenna

went to join her. "How much longer to dark?" she asked.

"Not long."

"Have they said anything new about that front?"

"It's speeded up." Carol reached over and took Brenna's hand in hers. They stood together, waiting.

Shane glanced at the radio—again. He kept telling himself that it made more sense to wait. The reality was that he could be days away from rescue. The batteries had to be conserved. But the temptation to try again was immense. It was as though some force outside himself was pushing him in that direction.

Reluctantly, he picked up the radio and switched it on. The all-too-familiar static answered him. Slowly, drawing on his rapidly fading strength, he spoke: "Anchorage Tower, this is Aleut niner-four-niner, do you read?"

There was no response. He started to turn the radio off but hesitated. It couldn't hurt to try for just a few more minutes.

"Anchorage Tower, pilot down, repeat pilot down. This is Aleut niner-four-niner. Come in."

Nothing. He was crazy to be doing this. It was a waste of time and besides, he could barely hold on to the radio. When had it gotten so heavy?

Or was it that he was getting so weak?

That grim thought focused his concentration. He took a breath, ignoring the pain that had recently appeared in his chest, and spoke again.

"Anchorage Tower, come in. Pilot down, repeat pilot down."

"Aleut ... tower ... wrong ... position ... must have ..."

Shane froze. After all the hours of listening for any indication that they actually knew he was alive, and there it was. One precious word. Aleut.

For just a moment, tears blurred his vision. Up until that instant, he hadn't allowed himself to acknowledge the full, terrible weight of solitude he had felt being alone, injured and cut off from the rest of the world. Now it exploded within him. But even as it did, he pushed it aside.

"Anchorage Tower, this is Aleut niner-four-niner, I'm reading you but barely. Say again."

He held his breath, hardly daring to hope there would be a response. When it came, it was almost entirely clear.

"Aleut niner-four-niner, this is Anchorage Tower. We are receiving you but poorly. Important you know your coordinates are believed wrong. Search has been unsuccessful. Vital we determine your position. Do you comp?"

"Yes!" He almost yelled it into the mike. "I comp, tower. Coordinates wrong. I comp. Say position rescue craft."

"Aleut niner...still breaking up..."

Dammit, not again! He needed them in the clear, just for a few more minutes.

"...ETA only known coordinates.... Say again, ETA... We need you to signal. Repeat, you must signal."

"When! Repeat, Tower, repeat ETA. Say again, repeat ETA."

"Aleut...can't...do you... Aleut..."

Contact was broken.

Shane sagged, exhausted. He had come so close. Frustration filled him and with it something very close to despair.

But he would not yield to it. He could not. Everything in him, everything that made him a man, refused to surrender. Fighting intense pain that seemed to be trying to swallow him whole, he opened the flap of the survival tent and dragged himself outside.

The rescue choppers were in the air. That much he had gotten. But he had no idea when they would be anywhere near his area. It might be in several minutes or several hours.

If he stayed in the tent, he could risk missing the only indication he might get.

Bundled against the bitter cold, he turned his face to the dying sun and waited.

"...Repeat, Tower...Say again, repeat...."

Contact was broken.

"Did he get it?" Dieter demanded. The contact with Shane had sent an electric bolt through the control tower. It had come suddenly, without warning, and faded just as quickly.

Brenna had a hand to her mouth, trying desperately not to cry. He sounded so weak. Nothing less than a terrible injury could have done that to him. Night was coming, another storm—

"Oh, God," she murmured, "please..."

"I don't know," Carl admitted. "He was breaking

up at this end and we were probably breaking up at his. I just can't say.''

"Try to raise him again and dammit, I have got to have some new coordinates *now*." Dieter pulled a battered cigar from his pocket, stuck it in his mouth and glared.

"Shane's hurt…really hurt…." Brenna murmured.

Carol put an arm around her. "He's going to be okay, honey. He's a strong man and they're going to get to him in time. Hang on."

But even as she spoke, she looked at the clock. Brenna looked with her. They both knew time was running out.

Chapter 19

Thursday, three days earlier...

The phone was ringing. Brenna opened her eyes blearily and stared into the darkness. The clock on the bedside table said 2:33 a.m. Who could possibly be calling at that hour?

Shane reached an arm over her and snagged the receiver. Through the lingering fog of dreams, she marveled at how he always seemed to wake up completely alert and ready to go.

"Dutton," he said.

She watched as he listened. Was it her imagination or did his face tighten?

"When?...Right...Got it. I'll be there in twenty minutes." He hung up and immediately swung his legs over the side of the bed.

"Be where?" Brenna asked. "It's the middle of the night."

Reaching for the pants he'd discarded rather suddenly several hours before, he said, "There's a tanker in trouble offshore. Looks to be going down."

That was a shame but what did it have to do with him?

"I don't—"

He was putting on his shirt, buttoning it quickly. "There are twelve men on board. The seas are real bad. If they take to the lifeboats, some of them aren't going to make it."

How else did you get off a ship that was going down? What other choices were there and why was Shane—

He stopped, looked at her gently, and said, "Honey, before I ran nice little airlines where I mostly get to be a desk jockey, I was a chopper pilot. I flew search-and-rescue. You know that."

"That was before, during the Gulf War...."

"It was the whole time I was in the Navy and I still do it—when there's need."

She sat up in the bed, drawing the covers with her. He had his boots on and was ready to go. "You mean—"

Looming over her, he put a hand under her chin, turned her face up to him, and kissed her hard. "I mean I'll be back in time for dinner. Pick out someplace nice to go, okay?"

And he was gone, out into the darkness. For just a moment, when he opened the front door, she heard the wind howling. Then he shut it behind him with a click that made her feel suddenly and horribly alone.

Fully awake, Brenna drew her knees up to her chin and rested her head on them. Even with the windows closed, she was aware of the storm. It was bad enough here. How much worse would it be at sea?

And how was anyone expected to pilot a helicopter through it?

There was no possibility of going back to sleep. She knew better than to even try. Getting up, she put on her robe and went downstairs. A glance out the window gave her a glimpse of tree branches lashed by snow and rain mixed together.

Shivering, she rummaged around in the cupboard and pulled out a container of herbal tea. As she fixed a cup, questions darted through her mind.

She and Shane had been dating for almost two months. How was it that in all that time, he hadn't mentioned that he happened to do something besides run Air Aleut? Had it never occurred to him to tell her that every once in a while he got back into a helicopter and flew into very dangerous conditions in an effort to save other people's lives?

She knew he was a man who didn't trot his achievements out for other people to admire. He'd been very uncomfortable when Bob had tried to tell her about the medal he'd won in the Gulf War. She respected his feelings but he should also have respected hers.

She'd told him about her father. He knew how she felt about loving someone whose life was on the line. He knew—and he hadn't said anything.

Anger spiraled through her. She pushed it down, ashamed to acknowledge it. Shane was doing something courageous and noble. What right did she have to berate him for it, even in her own thoughts?

But he should have told her. In almost two months, knowing what he knew about her past, he should have said something. At least that way, she would have been prepared. She wouldn't be standing there in the middle of the night, shocked and worried, not knowing what to think or feel.

He should have told her.

But he hadn't and she would just have to deal with that. With her cup of tea in hand, she went into the living room and flipped on the television. Just then, she needed to hear the sound of other people's voices.

Somewhere between an infomercial for a psychic hotline and a cooking show that seemed to focus entirely on things to do with chopped meat, Brenna dozed off. She woke to the gray light of predawn.

And the early morning news.

A blow-dried news reader straight out of central casting smiled into the camera and said, "Good morning, Alaska, and welcome to the Wake-Up news. I'm Jim Jameson. With me this morning are Tiffany Thompson and everybody's favorite weather guy, Bill Lieberwitz. We'll be getting to Bill in just a minute but first—"

His smile switched to a look of controlled but significant concern, indicated by a rippling of his slightly tanned forehead. "The tanker, *Red Star,* is floundering in heavy seas fifteen miles offshore. Conditions are so bad that her twelve-man crew is unable to launch lifeboats. Rescue helicopters at the scene are being buffeted by winds gusting to hurricane strength. Cameraman Luis Chang is on board one of them. Let's go to him live. Luis, are you there?"

The camera cut to a view of gray, surging water framed by the window of a helicopter. A voice that sounded as though it were being bounced up and down on a roller coaster said, "Uh, yeah, I'm here, Jim. Got to say, I wish I wasn't. Conditions here are terrible. Down below, you can see the tanker, *Red Star*—"

The camera panned over to the long shape of a tanker listing far to port.

"As you can see, she's in real danger of being swamped at any moment. Efforts are underway to get her crew off before that happens but with the wind gusts, it's extremely difficult to get in close enough to reach them. It's also very dangerous. One miscalculation will send a chopper straight into the sea."

On the steeply angled deck of the tanker, the shapes of men could be seen. They looked extraordinarily small and vulnerable against the raging fury all around them. It was difficult to see how they could possibly survive.

As the camera watched—and Brenna with it—one helicopter moved closer. The wind tore at it, slowing it down so much that it appeared to barely crawl forward, yet it kept coming. Several times, it dropped suddenly in a steep, erratic descent that seemed barely under control, if that.

"I can't overstate the risk here, Jim," Luis was saying. "The deck of that tanker is pitching in every direction. The wind turbulence is incredible. Getting those guys off there is going to take a miracle.''

''Any idea who's piloting that chopper, Luis?'' Jim asked. The camera cut back to him in the studio momentarily. He and Tiffany both looked just desperately, sincerely concerned.

Luis said something off to the side. Another voice replied but Brenna couldn't make it out.

''Guy's name is Shane Dutton,'' Luis said. ''Flew in the Gulf War. I'm just being told that he snagged more downed pilots than anybody else. Apparently has a reputation for being willing to fly through anything.''

Luis broke off, concentrating on keeping his camera as close to steady as he was going to get it.

Brenna sat frozen on the couch, unable to believe what she was seeing. The chopper pitched down again, seeming to scrape against the sea. She moaned and put her hand to her mouth. At the last possible moment, the aircraft pulled up. Relentlessly, despite the wind's worst efforts, it continued to move closer to the deck of the tanker. As the camera zoomed in for a tighter shot, she could make out the face of man at the controls.

Shane looked absolutely calm. There wasn't a flicker to his expression that indicated anything was even remotely wrong. He might have been sitting across the dinner table from her.

The camera moved down and she saw the terrified faces of the men gazing up at their only possible salvation. As she watched, a door opened on the side of the chopper and a cable began to descend.

"He's going for them," Luis said. She could hear the astonishment in his voice and knew it accurately reflected the extreme danger of the attempt. "If they rush that cable, their weight..."

"Oh, God," she murmured.

A savage gust tore at the tanker and chopper both. The deck listed further. Great waves of water washed over it. One of the men lost his grip on the pole he'd been holding on to. He was almost over the side when another just barely managed to grab him.

Shane moved closer. The cable dangled.

The nearest man snared it. Instantly, the cable began to rise. A second man lunged after the first and grabbed hold of his leg. Together, the two rose into the air.

"Hold on," Jim murmured. He caught himself and added, "For anyone just joining us, we're live at the scene of an incredible rescue attempt fifteen miles offshore where the tanker, *Red Star,* is floundering. Despite hurricane force wind gusts, one helicopter has managed to get into position to lift men off the tanker deck. The first two—yes! The first two are aboard the chopper. That's incredible. I really didn't think that—?"

"Another pilot's trying a run in," Luis interrupted, "but he's—"

In the camera's eye, a helicopter was caught in a sudden, tearing fury of wind and thrown toward the sea. At the last possible moment, it managed to pull up. But the pilot was clearly shaken. He drew back and regained altitude, but did not make another run at the tanker.

And still Shane stayed in position over the deck. The cable began to descend again.

"I can't imagine what it's taking to hold on like that," Luis said. "The wind is throwing these choppers around with tremendous violence. The best pilot in the world is taking a tremendous chance trying to fight it."

As he spoke, another man caught hold of the cable. Again, a second went with him. Moments later, they were reeled inside the chopper. The camera caught sight of them, crouched inside, peering down at the others who still remained.

The cable was lowered again.

At the same time, another chopper attempted to move in. Once again, the pilot could not keep control. He also barely avoided crashing into the sea.

"You've got to give them credit," Luis said. "They're all trying. But it looks like only one is making it so far. He's got four of the crew on board so far and it looks like two more are going up now."

Even as he spoke, a third man hurled himself at the cable. He got the leg of another and held tight.

The chopper began to list.

"That's too much," Jim said. He spoke with his usual patented authority.

"He'll get them all killed," Tiffany chimed in. Her cheerleader perfect features were perilously close to frowning.

"Shut up," Brenna said. She'd gotten up, without realizing it, and was standing directly in front of the television, her eyes locked on the desperate struggle being waged before her.

With agonizing slowness, the chopper straightened. The cable rose.

It occurred to her then that she wasn't the only one watching this. People all over Alaska and even elsewhere were tuning in to catch the morning headlines and seeing this instead.

Would they stop what they were doing? Put down that cup of coffee, and wait to see if men lived or died?

Or would they just shrug and go on about their business, as though it had nothing at all to do with them?

The cable was lowered again.

"We're staying with this," Jim said. "But just to let you commuters know, traffic looks fine, no problems, and this storm we're seeing is due to blow out later today. Now back live to Luis Chang and the tanker, *Red Star*. Luis, I gotta tell you, that's great camera work you're doing."

"Thanks," Luis said dryly. "Remind me when I get back to apply for your job."

Jim chuckled. "You know, buddy, I'd almost think you'd deserve it after what I'm seeing there. But hang in, looks like a couple more are going up."

It took twenty more minutes to get the last of the men off the tanker's deck. In that time, the other chopper pilots made repeated attempts to get into position to help Shane. None was able to do it. The extremely violent and unpredictable winds defeated them. It was all they could do to avoid going into the sea.

"That's the last," Luis said as the final man disappeared into the chopper. "And not a moment too soon—" His voice, weary with the strain of his own efforts, took on a note of awe. Even as the chopper door slammed shut, a wall of water washed over the deck of the *Red Star*. The tanker gave a massive shudder, held absolutely still for a moment, and then flipped over.

"Oh, my," Tiffany murmured.

"She's going down," Jim announced, making it official. He smiled into the camera. "That was truly amazing, wasn't it? We've been live at the site of the sinking of the tanker, *Red Star,* fifteen miles offshore. In a daring rescue, the twelve-man crew was snatched to safety by a death-defying helicopter pilot, Shane Dutton, who braved hurricane force winds to bring his craft within no more than a hundred feet of the pitching deck of the tanker. Risking his own life repeatedly, he managed to lift all of the twelve to safety moments before the *Red Star* was completely swamped and sank. We'll be back with more from cameraman, Luis Chang, who was on the scene. But first a word from our sponsors."

Cut to commercial.

A woman started singing about the freedom of the open road in a new something-or-other.

Brenna turned the television off. She picked up her tea. It was cold.

Just as well. She needed a good, hot jolt of serious coffee, not this herbal stuff.

Shane had done it. He'd flown into immense danger, saved twelve men from certain death, and managed not to get himself killed in the process.

She was weak with relief, profoundly glad, astounded and amazed.

And still angry.

Now that the immediate crisis was past, one thought remained uppermost in her mind—he should have told her.

Chapter 20

Friday

"**Y**ou should have told me."

It was the evening after the rescue. Between filling out reports, accepting the grateful thanks of the *Red Star*'s crew and fending off the media, Shane had been busy up until then. But he'd finally shaken loose and come over to Brenna's, intending to take her out to dinner.

Only to find that she was in no mood to do anything except "talk."

No, that wasn't fair. When he appeared at her front door, she flew into his arms, clinging to him, kissing him passionately, murmuring her great joy at his return.

He didn't doubt for a moment that all that was real.

But it wasn't all there was. After that initial explosion of relief, she withdrew from him, becoming suddenly wary and quiet.

"What is it?" he asked.

And then she said it, standing there in the hallway, wearing jeans and a soft pink knit sweater with her hair pulled back and no makeup on. She looked right at him and said, "You should have told me."

"Told you what?" It was a cheap ploy but he took it anyway. He needed time to regroup. His own emotions hadn't exactly had smooth sailing the past day.

"You know perfectly well what." Her temper flared. He watched the angry gleam creep into her eyes and smothered a sigh. Whatever dexterity he had with a helicopter, he sure as hell couldn't claim the same with a woman. At least, not with this woman.

"You should have told me you were still flying search-and-rescue missions."

"I don't fly them very often."

"Several times a year, at least that's what they said on the news when they finally got some background information on you. You flew in the Rocky Mountain fires last summer. Two years ago, you plucked a vulcanologist out of the heart of an erupting volcano on Oahu. He got his boots singed by the lava, it was that close! And you've flown more at-sea rescues than most full-time search pilots. So just what exactly do you mean by not very often?"

"What am I supposed to do?" he asked quietly. "Say no?"

"Did that ever occur to you?"

"Refuse to help? Let men die because I had something better to do rather than go after them? No, that has never occurred to me."

"Other pilots seem to have a sense of their own limitations. You can't tell me they don't. I watched what happened out there, Shane. I watched every minute of it, and I saw those other pilots pull back when they realized it was too much for them."

"For them," he said. "Not for me."

"Oh, I see. You're the guy who will fly through anything. Nothing's too much for you."

"It's not like that," he insisted. "I'm not some kid who has to prove something. I know what I can do and what I can't. It's a judgment call."

"Like it was when my father went into that alley."

"I'm not your father! I don't put my life on the line every day."

"Just several times a year."

He shook his head, not believing he was hearing this. He hadn't expected the hero treatment, but he'd thought she'd be glad when he turned up. Instead, she was madder than hell and blaming him.

"Look, what is it exactly you object to? That I didn't ask your permission? We don't own each other, Brenna."

She flinched visibly but she didn't back down, not even a little. "I never said we did, but I'm beginning to think we don't even know each other. I opened up to you, I told you what happened in my past and how I felt about it. You must have realized then that what you do would have an impact on me but you still didn't see fit to mention it."

"And what if I had? What would your reaction have been?"

"At least I would have been prepared. It wouldn't have come as such a shock."

"And that's it? Nothing else?"

"I don't know—" she admitted. "I can't say since I never got the chance."

"The chance to back away, not to get yourself involved with someone who someday just might do something that could possibly put him in some danger. That's what you would have done. You would have backed off just like you did with that cop."

"That was different! I wasn't in love with—" She broke off and turned away from him.

"And you are in love with me? Is that what you're saying?" He took hold of her and spun her around. "Because of that, you think I should give up who I am just so you'll feel safe?"

"Go to hell."

His hand tightened on her arm. He felt it happening and stopped immediately, but the damage was done. Very quietly, Brenna said, "You're hurting me."

"I'm sorry, I didn't mean to—"

"I know you didn't. You're not the kind of man who would ever do that. But it happens anyway and you can't seem to understand that. I sat there, Shane, through every moment. I listened to Luis and Jim and Tiffany spell it all out in loving detail. I saw what almost happened to those other pilots and I realized full well what could happen to you at any second."

She touched a hand to his face in a gesture that was filled with tender regret. "You were magnificent.

You saved twelve lives. I know that and I think it's wonderful. But in the time we've been together, with all we've shared, you never saw fit to warn me, to prepare me in any way. You know what that says to me? That you kept the most important part of yourself separate, as though what happened between us didn't have anything at all to do with your real life.''

"What happened between us might never have happened at all if I'd been completely frank with you. You just admitted that yourself.''

"And you did want it to happen, so you didn't tell me anything that could interfere. You took away a choice that should have been mine.''

"Then take it back. Make the choice but make it now because I'm not going to apologize for who I am or what I do. You're just going to have to accept that.''

"Or not.''

Their eyes met. Quietly, Shane said, "Or not.''

She did hesitate. He got that much at least. But her voice was steady when she said, "I can't accept it. You're giving me an ultimatum, just go along with the way things are no matter what that costs me. You say you aren't willing to give up who you are. Well, I'm not willing to give up who I am, either.''

"That doesn't leave us a whole lot of room to maneuver.''

"No, it doesn't.''

Her throat was so tight she could barely breathe. Pain surged through her. She was lost, afraid, more uncertain of anything than she had ever been in her life. Desperate, hardly knowing what she was saying, she gasped, "Just go. Leave me alone."

Shane stared at her for a long moment. His hand tightened on the door knob. Without emotion he said, "I'll give you a call in a few days."

She nodded but didn't speak. A moment longer, he looked at her. A deep well of regret and confusion was opening up within him. He'd never felt anything like it. But then he'd never been in a situation like this. He'd never cared for a woman as he did for Brenna but at the same time, he'd also never felt so close to losing himself. It was not a pleasant sensation.

He stepped out into the night. Behind him, the door clicked shut.

Sunday

He should have said—

Shane jerked back to consciousness suddenly. How long had he been asleep? Good, healthy fear roared through him. Could he have missed the choppers?

After several moments, his heartbeat returned to normal. He had dozed off but only briefly. Okay, now that he knew it could happen, he'd stay alert for it. Scooping up snow with one hand, he pressed it against his face. The cold gave him the shock he needed but he didn't mistake it for actual strength. That was just about gone.

But the memory of that argument with Brenna lingered. Why hadn't he given her the slightest reassurance? He wasn't that hard-edged a person. He knew how to compromise when there was a reason for doing it. So why hadn't he?

Because you were scared.

Unbidden, some completely separate part of his mind spoke.

"Like hell," Shane murmured. He stirred restlessly.

She'd gotten too close.

Who *was* this obnoxious part of himself? Where was this stuff coming from? He didn't have any problem with Brenna being too close. The closer the better.

This isn't about sex.

Oh, great, now it turned out not only did he suddenly seem to have developed a very annoying alter ego, but it didn't have the sense God gave a gnat.

"It's always about sex."

Oh, right. You never once thought she was smart, or funny or just a good person. That never once went through your mind. All you ever wanted to do was—

"I don't believe this!" It had to be the fever. He groped in the pack, found a couple more analgesics and swallowed them.

I'm still here.

"You're...I'm—"

Confusing, isn't it? You know, she was just afraid something like this could happen. Maybe we should have listened to her.

"I'm being second-guessed by myself. Great."

I'm not happy about it either but she did have a

point. I, you, we—whatever—never seriously consid-
ered that death was an actual option.

"Right, I flew all those missions in the war and
never once thought about getting killed."

You thought about not getting killed. That's differ-
ent.

"This is different—"

Bingo.

Different. What was different was that he had to
face up to the possibility that he really might not get
out of this one alive. A few times, during the war and
on some of the rougher rescues since then, he'd been
in situations where the idea that he might die had at
least flitted through his mind. But there hadn't been
any time to think about it and by the time there was,
it was over and gone.

But this was different. He was getting plenty of
opportunity to contemplate his own mortality.

So that was how it must have looked from Brenna's
point of view. Too bad he hadn't realized it sooner.

Instead, he'd walked out on her. Oh, sure, he'd
meant to call "in a few days," like he said. But what
good did that do, now? There was no particular reason
to think he was going to get the chance. And if he
didn't—

Then her last memory of him would be of a real
jerk who wasn't man enough to care about her feelings. Some nice way to be remembered by the woman
he'd wanted to sit on the porch and watch the sunsets
with.

Hey, whatta you, giving up?

"Like hell." He wrestled himself into a sitting position and kept his eyes on the sky. If he was going out, he wasn't going to let it be easy.

Chapter 21

Sunday

The hands of the clock seemed to be frozen. The more Brenna stared at them, the less they moved until now they appeared to have stopped entirely. Her eyes hurt. She looked away only to find the afterimage of the clock floating in front of her, as though burned into her brain.

The faces of the men in the control tower were unbearably strained. She couldn't look at them any longer, either.

Wearily, she closed her eyes. A single tear slid down her cheek. She whispered soundlessly, "Forgive me."

If only time could be turned back. If only she could have another chance. If only—

She had thought only of herself. In her pride, she had failed to consider anyone else. And because of that, she had sent Shane from her, hurt and angry.

It had all seemed so obvious. He "should" have told her. He "should" have considered her feelings. He "should" have given her a choice. And that was all still true, but it was not the whole of truth.

The rest of it was that she was there, in the control tower, waiting—a woman desperately afraid that the man she loved would never return to her alive. And as she did, other men were out searching for him. They were pushing their choppers and themselves to the limit, straining fuel reserves, risking being caught far from any safe landing if bad weather moved in again, unwilling to give up while there was still a chance that he might live.

Whatever happened, she would never be able to adequately tell them how much she appreciated what they were doing. And yet she had blamed Shane for doing exactly the same thing for others.

Those men on the *Red Star* had families. There were other women—and children—who had been spared terrible grief because of what Shane did. Because of what he risked.

And she had blamed him—

Another tear fell. She swallowed hard and rubbed the back of her hand against her cheek. If only she had thought more, if she hadn't been so focused on her own feelings. If she had just seen it even a little from his perspective.

But she hadn't. And now there might never be another chance. She reached in her pocket, found a tissue and blew her nose. Breaking down wasn't going to do anyone any good. Somehow, she had to find the strength to hold herself together. But it was so hard. The waiting and the not knowing were taking a terrible toll.

And yet, despite that, deep inside her, something hard and knotted began to loosen. When she raised her head long moments later, she was very far from any sense of rightness. But she did feel within her the beginning of acceptance. She would find the strength to face whatever was to come. It might be the final gift she would give to Shane's memory, but give it she would.

Her gaze caught the wall clock. As she watched, the hands moved.

Waves of dark and light moved over Shane. He fought against them, clinging to the outer edges of consciousness. The pain in his leg was very close to causing him to black out. With every breath he drew, his chest rattled.

One way or another, this was going to be over soon.

It was time to face that. Really face it.

He reached under the blankets and withdrew the small pocket calendar from his jacket. This early in the year, there were still plenty of empty pages. He was so weak that he could barely hold the pen. Slowly, painfully, he wrote.

When he was done, he closed the notebook and slipped it back into his pocket. A deep sense of relief filled him. It would have been so very simple to just sink into that relief and let go of everything else. Only the thought of Brenna stopped him. He didn't want a letter to have to speak for him to her. He wanted to be able to do that himself.

But darkness seemed to be closing in around the edges of his vision. He knew he had very little time left. Oddly, he felt more at peace than he'd expected. He thought of people he loved—his parents, and brothers and sisters—good friends in the service and out—the things he'd done and the things he hoped to.

Mostly, he thought about Brenna. They were good thoughts despite the regret for what had not been. He couldn't explain it, but he felt very close to her just then. She was hundreds of miles away and yet it was almost as though she lay beside him. He imagined he could feel her warmth, the soft rhythm of her heart, the comfort of her nearness.

She snored—

Well, she did. Not the bed rattling kind of snoring, just little puffs of sound. He probably did the same himself. Little puff-puffs, steady and regular, but deeper than usual, funny somehow, not really like her.

More like an engine.

His eyes opened. He stared into a sky where thick, gray clouds obscured the first stars. A flake of snow drifted down and settled on his brow. Another followed. Within minutes, eddies of snow whirled in the suddenly sharp wind.

The cold numbed him. His pain, so constant a presence, seemed diminished. He wanted nothing so much as to close his eyes and let the darkness take him.

Except that engine sure made a racket.

Engine? What engine? From the depths of oblivion, Shane climbed just far enough to realize that what he heard was no fever-induced fantasy. It was real.

He didn't think, didn't hesitate, didn't do anything except grab for the survival pack. The flare slipped from between his fingers. For a horrible moment, it seemed he would lack the strength to light it. From a reserve so deep he had never known it existed, he summoned the very last of the life force that was himself.

The prayer he murmured as he struck the fuse climbed to heaven on a column of fire, hung for an timeless moment, and exploded.

Brenna opened her eyes. She saw Dieter gripping the mike in his big hand. "Say again!"

From the lead rescue chopper, Frank spoke with fierce relief. "Flare sighted, approximately three miles northwest this position. Turning."

There was silence for several moments.

Under his breath, Bob murmured, "It's almost dark."

"And the front's here," Carl said. "They're going to get hit."

"Fuel?" Dieter demanded.

"They can stay on post another thirty minutes. Then they've got to be out of there."

Dieter spoke into the mike again. "Frank, you're going to have to make this real fast."

No response.

"You're in the edge of that front now. Fuel reserves give you thirty minutes, no more."

Nothing.

"Dammit," Dieter muttered. "Answer me."

"We're a little busy here," Frank replied, finally. "I think I can see traces of where a plane could have hit. Treetops are sheared off. It looks like a straight shot to a cleft in the hills up ahead." Silence again, and then, "There! Wreckage sighted, repeat wreckage sighted. Going in."

"Home stretch," Bob said. He gave Brenna a smile belied by the look that passed between him and Carol.

Softly, Carol said, "C'mon, honey, let's sit down."

Brenna stared at her for a moment uncomprehendingly, then did as she said. Silence descended on the control tower. No one moved or spoke.

In the breathless silence, the crack of the radio sounded like a rifleshot.

"Anchorage Tower—we have recovery. Repeat, we have him."

Ninety minutes later, the airport closed again. The rapidly moving storm left no choice. But no one left the control tower. All eyes remained on the runway. Ambulance and police escort were already in position. So were several emergency vehicles. There was no guarantee that the landings would be smooth.

"They're five miles out," Carl said quietly.

Bob held out his hand to Brenna. "Time to go."

She stood. He helped her on with her coat. Carol put a soft wool scarf over her head and tied it gently beneath her chin. "You okay?" she asked.

Brenna nodded. She felt strangely calm. Turning to Dieter and all the others, she said simply, "Thank you."

Several of the men blinked hard. None was unmoved. They murmured their hopes, their blessings. Bob took her arm. They walked out through the terminal, now almost empty. Passengers who hadn't made it out earlier had given up. Only a few exhausted castaways slumped in the hard plastic chairs.

A security guard opened the door to the tarmac and stood aside for them to pass. The cold hit them at once. Stinging snow whipped their faces. The wind was so strong that just moving forward was a struggle.

"We can wait in the ambulance," Bob said.

Brenna shook her head. "You go. I need the fresh air." He didn't move and she relented because she realized he would feel honor bound to stay with her. But once in the back of the ambulance, she crouched near the door, watching.

"It won't be much longer," Bob said. "They'll come in on instruments. It'll be fine."

The white lines of tension around his mouth said he feared otherwise. Brenna put her hand over his and gave him a reassuring smile. He was being so kind to her but she realized fully that she wasn't the only person hurting. They all were. To varying degrees to be sure, but hurting still.

"It'll be fine," she repeated as though saying it could make it so.

A flicker of light shone through the thick clouds. It vanished, reappeared and grew stronger. A small chopper suddenly emerged, seeming to hurtle toward the runway.

Brenna held her breath. The aircraft looked so

small and fragile against the power of the storm. It hovered an instant then touched the ground only to bounce right off. An instant later, it came down again and this time stayed.

The other choppers in the rescue squad were landing one after another, but Brenna was barely aware of them. She saw nothing but the grim face of the man hovering at the open door. The propellers were still churning as he jumped onto the tarmac. Behind him, she caught a glimpse of a stretcher.

The medics ran forward. She and Bob followed but more slowly. Partly, she was simply frozen with fear, so much so that she could no longer even feel the cold. But also, she had the sense not to get in the way.

Frank was shouting. She had to strain to hear him.

"Temp's 104, breathing rapid and erratic, lungs bad, we've had him on oxygen all the way. Left leg is broken, probable septicemia. BP low and falling. Suspected head injury. I'd say he's concussed but we can't tell for sure."

The medics were nodding. They'd been in radio contact with Frank and knew most of this, but the update was important. It was accomplished in the minute or so it took to hand off the stretcher.

"Conscious at all?" one of the medics asked.

Frank shook his head. "He was trying to say something at one point but I couldn't catch it."

Brenna stared at the still figure lying on the stretcher. His head was in a brace, his face almost covered by the oxygen mask. The rest of him was beneath survival blankets. An IV snaked under them into his arm. Except for the mane of blond hair stark against the stretcher, she couldn't have known it was Shane.

Her throat clogged. She sucked in air, fighting with all her strength not to cry, and followed the stretcher into the back of the ambulance.

Chapter 22

Sunday

Why did every hospital smell the same? Was it something they used to clean with? And the coffee...why couldn't they make decent coffee? Surely, they had enough practice.

Brenna put down the cup of coffee not even she could drink and closed her eyes. She was so tired that the moment her lids closed she could feel herself falling down a long, black hole. Another second and she would have been asleep, standing right there up against the wall. Horses could do it, why couldn't she? For all she knew, she already had.

What stopped her was the sound of footsteps coming to a halt in front of her. Slowly, as though lifting weights, she opened first one eye and then the other.

A middle-aged man was watching her. He wore a white coat and a watchful expression. A stethoscope dangled around his neck.

"I'm Dr. Mathieson. Are you Mrs. Dutton?"

She swallowed past the lump in her throat. "We aren't married. I'm a...friend."

"I see." He gestured toward a small waiting room just off the corridor. "Let's sit down."

When they had done so, Dr. Mathieson rubbed a hand over his face. He looked as though he stifled a yawn. "Sorry, it's been a long night. Mr. Dutton has been moved from emergency to intensive care." He looked at her for a moment. She supposed he saw the exhausted eyes and behind them, the fear. His expression softened. "Are you alone here?"

Brenna shook her head. "Two friends are with me but they're getting a bite to eat. I just needed some time to myself."

"Okay. Has Mr. Dutton's family been notified?"

She told him what Bob had told her. "Yes, and they're trying to get here but the weather has them delayed in Seattle."

"I hope it clears soon. Look, this is the situation. Mr. Dutton has septicemia. That's a bacteria infection of the blood. It apparently started when his leg was broken during the crash. The rescue team found evidence that he had used an antibiotic from the emergency pack but it doesn't appear to have worked. That's a problem these days. We've put him on an IV with something we hope will do the job better."

"Hope?"

He lowered his eyes for a moment but caught himself and looked at her straight on again. "He's in bad shape. Besides the septicemia, he's got pneumonia in both lungs and a concussion. There are also some problems from exposure and dehydration although he appears to have avoided the worst of that. Overall, his condition is critical. He's on life support, including a ventilator."

"I see—" She didn't really. The whole thing was incomprehensible. Shane was so alive, so strong, so intensely connected to the world. It was just barely possible to think of him leaving it in a sudden blaze, gone in an instant because of an accident. But to think of him dying slowly, succumbing to disease…that was too much.

"I'm sorry," the doctor said gently. "But frankly, if he hadn't been in top-notch shape to start with, he would never have made it this far. If he can make it through the next twenty-four to forty-eight hours…"

"I'd like to be with him."

"All right." He hesitated, then said, "If you feel like it, you could try talking to him. He's on some pretty powerful drugs and there's also the concussion, but there are times when a human connection seems to make a difference no matter what."

Was he serious or did he merely mean to offer her some hope, however faint?

Brenna followed the doctor out of the small room and up to intensive care. It was a separate unit, sealed off from everything else. The seriousness of the place was evident the moment she stepped into it. Half a dozen glassed-in cubicles surrounded a central nursing station. Here there was none of the easy coming and going of the rest of the hospital, only grim, intent purpose.

Her first sight of Shane was behind transparent walls. He lay in a narrow hospital bed. A mask covered his face. Wires and tubes protruded. As she watched, green lines flashed across a monitor near the bed, tracking his vital signs.

A nurse at the central station looked up, gave her a small smile, and went back to reading a chart.

"If you need anything…" Dr. Mathieson began.

She shook her head. "I'll be fine, thanks."

He left her then and walked over to the station to speak quietly with the nurse. Brenna hesitated. Slowly, she opened the sliding glass panel and stepped into the cubicle. The light was dimmer inside. Except for the soft beeping of the monitor and the rasp of the ventilator, it was very quiet.

There was a chair near the bed. She sat down in it and just stared at him for several moments. It was the ventilator that really forced her to confront the truth. His condition was so bad that he couldn't be counted on to breathe on his own.

They use ventilators all the time, she told herself. People come off them all the time.

And sometimes people are taken off, so that they can die in peace.

He wasn't going to die. Dammit, he wasn't!

She reached out and took Shane's hand in hers. His skin felt hot and dry. The fingers lay limply. She thought of his touch, the strength and sheer power of life that it always conveyed, and shut her eyes hard for a moment.

"Hi," she said softly. Her throat was thick. She took a breath and tried again. "It's me, Brenna. You're in the hospital. They're taking really good care of you. Your plane crashed but somehow you stayed alive until Frank and the others could find you. Somehow...I can't imagine how. Your leg was broken and there's an infection. You have pneumonia and a concussion, but you're going to be all right. You are..."

She stopped. Her chest hurt. She was beginning to understand why people spoke of heartache.

"I don't know if you can hear me," she went on, "but I'm staying. I won't leave you. Your family is coming but the weather's delayed them. It's supposed to start clearing tomorrow. That's in just a few hours."

His face was white under the mask. There was no response at all. She might as well have been talking to herself.

That didn't matter. If he didn't hear her, he didn't. But she wouldn't give up for anything.

Talk to him, Dr. Mathieson had said. The human connection could be important. Perhaps it could even be a lifeline of sorts, reaching into the unknown, giving a person something to grab hold of and follow back.

All right then, she'd try.

She bent closer, her lips brushing his cheek, speaking softly. "I'm so sorry, Shane. I shouldn't have said what I did, it was stupid and selfish. Please give me a chance to tell you that. Please don't leave."

Her voice broke. She caught herself, determined

not to put her pain and fear off on him. She was here to help, not burden him yet further.

"It's snowing again," she said. "I suppose that's good in the long run. Spring should be beautiful. You weren't here to see it begin last year, were you? It comes so slowly that you feel it will never arrive and then suddenly, it's there. The air softens and the snowdrops come up, those are flowers. People seem to walk more slowly and their hats come off. And the children... It's funny but in the winter I don't notice children very much. Oh, you see them every once in a while sledding or skating, but mostly they're all bundled up and stuck away in school. With the spring, they seem to appear again. I think of spring that way, coming on the sounds of children's voices. I leave my windows open so I can hear them."

It might have been her imagination but she could have sworn she felt a slight pressure from his fingers. It was gone in a moment but the impression lingered, and spurred her on.

"Do you know," she continued softly, "when I truly realized I had fallen in love with you? It was just about a month ago. We went skiing, remember? And afterward—"

One month earlier...

"That was so great," Brenna exclaimed. "I can't believe how great that was!"

Shane smiled modestly. "Glad you liked it."

"Liked it? It was the most incredible experience I've ever had and—" At the look on his face, she grinned. "Well, maybe not the absolutely most incredible but—"

"No, no, it's all right, you can say it. That's fine—really." He gave an exaggerated sigh. "You've got a thing for mountains. I can live with that."

"It's not like it was just any mountain," Brenna replied. She couldn't resist. They were standing at the foot of the most daring ski run she had ever attempted. Standing upright, no bones broken, everything intact. Incredible.

When he'd first proposed it, she'd tried to back off. She liked to ski but wasn't competitive about it. If he wanted to try the tougher runs, that was fine with her. They could meet back at the lodge. She was perfectly happy sticking with the runs she knew.

He'd insisted. She'd been skiing for almost ten years. She enjoyed doing it. She was ready for something a little more adventurous. He'd be beside her every foot of the way. She'd love it.

And she had. It was heart-pounding, adrenaline-rushing excitement, pure and simple. If it hadn't already been so late, she'd have been ready to do it again.

"It will be dark soon," she said with regret.

Shane nodded. He flicked a snowflake from her nose and grinned. "Race you to the hot cocoa." Without waiting, he was off. Brenna followed.

The day had been crisp and clear; night promised to be the same. Already, stars shone brilliantly overhead, a sea of them, endlessly beckoning. Most of the other skiers were already back at the lodge. They were alone on the trail with only the whisper of wind and the rhythm of their skis to punctuate silence that seemed infinite. Brenna smiled with the sheer pleasure of the moment, then redoubled her efforts to catch Shane.

He was fast—very, very fast—and she had no expectation of catching him. But after a few minutes, he slowed and waited until she came alongside. They skied the rest of the way to the lodge together.

Winter darkness came on quickly. The light had almost vanished and they could see the illuminated windows of the lodge when they heard the sound. Shane reacted first. He rammed his poles into the ground and came to an abrupt stop.

"What's that?"

Brenna had gone a little past him. She turned and came back. "What?"

"That sound. Listen."

For a moment, all she could hear was the sharp crack of a frozen twig and in the distance, very faintly, the beat of music from the lodge. Then she heard something altogether different. A cry.

"That," Shane said. "It sounded like—"

They looked at each other.

"A child," Brenna murmured. "But it can't be. A child wouldn't be out here alone and—"

The cry came again. Shane cursed under his breath and turned in its direction. They crested a small hillock just off the trail and stopped again, listening.

"Maybe we were wrong," Brenna said. "It could have been a bird of some kind—"

"It wasn't a bird." Shane raised his voice, calling.

"Can you hear me? We're trying to find you. Shout if you can hear me."

Through the darkness, almost muffled by a gust of wind, came a faint sob.

"That way," Shane said.

Twenty yards farther on, near a line of trees, they found her. She was about five years old, Brenna guessed, gaily dressed in a pink-and-purple ski jacket and pants. Her small face was pinched with cold, her eyes wide with fear. When she saw them, she pulled back into the shadow of a tree, as though trying to make herself invisible.

Shane bent down beside her. He spoke gently. "Hi, my name's Shane. What's yours?"

No answer. The child locked her lips tightly together and looked from one to the other of them.

"Let me guess," Shane said. "Your mommy and daddy told you not to speak to strangers. Is that right?"

The little girl nodded.

Brenna knelt down next to Shane. Very softly, she said, "We're going back to the lodge for hot cocoa. Would you like to come with us?"

Miserably, the little girl shook her head.

"The lodge is just on the other side of that hill," Shane pointed. "You must have wandered off and gotten lost. Is that what happened?"

"Y-yes..."

"People will be looking for you soon, if they aren't already. We could go back and tell them where you are but it's very cold and the sun has gone down. How about you just come with us?"

As he spoke, Shane reached out a hand to the little girl. Slowly, her eyes locked on his, she took it. "I'll bet you like piggyback rides," he said and swung her up on his shoulders. The motion caught her unawares. She squealed with delight and clung to him.

"So, how about telling us your name?" Shane said as they started off.

"Melanie." Gaining confidence rapidly on her high perch, she added, "I'm five. How old are you?"

"Thirty-five," Shane told her.

"You're almost as old as my daddy."

"Did he come skiing with you?"

"Yep, him and mommy, and some of their friends." Her voice dropped. "Am I in trouble? Are they going to be mad at me?"

"I think they'll just be happy to see you, honey," Brenna said. She glanced at Shane. His mouth was set in a hard, thin line.

"I hope so." She sounded doubtful. "Daddy's very busy. That's why we came here, so he could talk business with his friends. Mommy said I had to stay home with Alma."

"Who's Alma?" Shane asked. They were over the hillock and back on the trail to the lodge.

"She's my nanny. She comes from Ecuador. Do you know where that is?"

"Yes, as a matter of fact, I do. Is Alma here?"

"No, she stayed home. I cried and cried and begged mommy to bring me so finally she did but I was supposed to be good." A small sniffle escaped. "I wasn't good."

"Did you mean to get lost?" Brenna asked.

"No, honest, I didn't! I followed a squirrel, that's all. When I wanted to go back, I couldn't see which way. I thought they'd find me soon—" Her voice trailed off. She slumped against Shane, exhausted.

"Poor little kid," Brenna murmured.

Shane looked angry. "Where are her parents? Why aren't they out here looking for her? Dammit, how could anyone be so careless—"

He broke off as they reached the lodge. The main entrance was framed by large, timber doors twice as tall as a man. They stood open to reveal an inviting interior, carpeted by hand-woven rugs, the walls decorated with Inuit art and at the opposite end, an enormous fireplace aglow with flame.

Several people were standing near the entrance. There was a slender man of medium height with a blond woman next to him. Both looked as though they had stepped from the pages of a fashion catalog, except for their tense, strained expressions. They were talking urgently to a man in the burgundy blazer of a lodge manager.

"I was in a business meeting, but I'm telling you, my wife only turned her back for a moment and Melanie was gone. We thought she'd wandered off to the video room where we were earlier or maybe even the pool, but there's no sign of her."

"I wish you'd told me immediately," the other man said. "If it's possible she went outside—"

"She did," Shane said. He lifted Melanie down gently from his shoulders. She had dozed off and now awoke suddenly. Seeing her parents, she smiled hugely and held out her arms.

"Mommy, daddy, you're here!"

"Darling!" The blond woman choked back a sob and gathered her daughter up into her arms. Beside her, the father looked grimly relieved. "Thank God," he muttered.

"Or thank these two," the manager said. He shot a sharp look at the little family group, then asked, "Where did you find her?"

"On the other side of the hillock by the tree line," Shane replied. "She said she was following a squirrel and got lost."

"Thank you very much," the man said. "We were very worried."

"Oh, yes, thank you," the woman added. She was holding on to Melanie tightly. "We can't thank you enough."

"Sure you can," Shane said. "Make sure it doesn't happen again."

The man started to say something, saw the look on Shane's face, and apparently thought better of it. He gathered up his wife and child, and returned inside.

When they were gone, the manager let out a deep, slow breath. He slipped the cell phone he'd been about to use back into his pocket. Quietly, he asked, "Any idea how long she was out there?"

"She was very cold," Brenna said, "and scared. I don't think she would have gone off once it started to get dark so she must have been out there awhile, say at least an hour."

"And I hear about it now." He sighed. He shrugged, resigned. "I suppose we chalk this up to all's well that ends well."

"You don't sound so sure." A pulse beat in Shane's jaw. Brenna had never seen that happen before. She found it oddly fascinating.

"In another five minutes, we would have had an all-out search underway," the manager said. "Maybe we would have found her. I'd like to think so. And maybe we would have had the kind of tragedy I worry about too much."

"Too much?" Brenna asked.

He looked very tired. Maybe that was why he said more than he should have. "Do you have any idea how many missing kids we get? Two or three times a week isn't unusual. They wander off, the parents say. They can't understand what happened. Last month, the lifeguard spotted a three-year old at the pool on his own. When we asked the parents why they weren't watching him, they said they just stopped off at the room to pick up a couple of things. C'mon, it takes maybe two minutes for a kid that age to drown."

He managed a crooked smile. "The funny thing is, we aren't even a family-type resort. We get mainly couples like you or business meetings. The last place I worked—" He broke off, suddenly recollecting himself. "Sorry. Again, thank you very much. Why don't you stop by the bar? I'd be happy to arrange for a complimentary cocktail."

"We'll pass," Shane said. He took Brenna's arm. They were halfway across the lobby before he slowed down. "I can't believe that. I absolutely cannot believe that."

"Thank God you heard her."

"Right, but what if I hadn't? What kind of parents would just let something like that happen?"

"According to the manager, more and more of them."

He shook his head, disgusted. "I don't get this. I have three younger brothers and sisters. My parents didn't always have it easy. My mom went back to work to make sure we'd have the money to get through college. I started dinner plenty of times and did my share of grocery shopping. None of that hurt me any, far from it. But dammit, they knew where I was. They knew what I was doing. They especially knew it when I was five years old!"

"She's all right," Brenna said softly. "You heard her, you found her, and she's going to be fine."

"Until the next time."

"Maybe there won't be a next. Did you see the look on her mother's face?"

"No," he acknowledged. "I was too busy wanting to punch out her father. Business meetings! I run my own business. I know what it's like to spend way too much time in meetings. But she's just a kid...."

"The mother looked like she couldn't decide whether to cry or scream. I think it really got to her."

"Good. I hope she has nightmares about it. I hope she wakes up screaming *and* crying. And I hope she makes sure her husband never hears the end of it. Every day kids are being—"

"Shane," she said gently, "let it go. Melanie will be all right. Who knows, maybe this will save her from something that could have been a lot worse."

He took a deep breath and let it out slowly. "I'm

sorry. It's just that I like kids. One of my sisters has two and I've been getting to know them. They're really...interesting."

Brenna looked at him quizzically. "I've heard people use a lot of words to describe kids but I don't remember that one."

"They really are. They look at things differently, without all the preconceived ideas we carry around. They're enthusiastic, they care. And their curiosity is wonderful. You can't beat that."

"You like kids."

"What's not to like? They're in the same league as puppies and kittens, cute and helpless."

"It's not the same. Kids mean a lot more work."

"They're worth it."

He said that with such conviction that she stopped right in front of the elevators and looked at him. With the tone of one who has just made a significant discovery, she said, "You want to have children."

He raised his hands defensively. "Hey, I didn't say this minute."

"But you do."

"Someday, sure. Don't you?"

She'd never really thought about it. No, that wasn't true. She'd thought about thinking about it someday. When she got around to it. When she hit thirty. When she might be running out of time.

All the sudden, it was someday.

"I like children," she said carefully.

"In the abstract or a little more concretely?"

"The thing is, I don't actually know any children. My older brother got married, but now he's divorced and there weren't any kids, which was a good thing. As far as my friends go, none of them have kids yet although I suppose some of them are thinking about it."

"Never mind them. What do you think?"

She hesitated. "I think I was promised hot cocoa, so where is it?"

He punched the elevator button. "Does it scare you that much?"

"Scare me? Of course not. Why would kids scare me?"

"Well, first there's the whole pregnancy and labor thing. Then they're actually here and you have to take care of them. They don't sleep, they want to be fed all the time, they scream like crazy and they produce stuff in their diapers that you would not believe. And that's while they're still babies. Then they're walking, talking, feeding themselves, having conversations, and you start to relax a little. But then along comes Puberty, capital *P,* and you get to go through it all over again."

She stared at him in amazement. "You really have thought about this."

"Terrifying, isn't it?"

"Oh, I don't know. You haven't quite convinced me to get my tubes tied."

"Really? You'd still consider it?"

"Hey, I didn't say this minute."

"It's not something to rush into," he agreed. The elevator came. They stepped in. As he pushed the floor button, Shane gathered her to him. Against her hair, he said, "But there's no harm in practicing."

She tipped her head back and teased, "You want to borrow a kid?"

He put both arms around her, his hands stroking her back to the curve of her buttocks. "Actually, I was thinking of the prekid part of the process."

"Oh, *that* part." She moved against him slowly, seductively and was rewarded by his instant response. "Do I still get cocoa?"

"We'll see," he said and took her mouth with his.

Chapter 23

Sunday

What was happening to him? He'd been out again. What if he'd missed the choppers? They were coming, he'd heard something and then—

Dammit, why couldn't he move? What was going on—?

Panic coursed through him. He was aware, sort of, but seemingly disconnected from his body. It was as though his consciousness were in one place and everything else in another. That couldn't be, unless—

Was he dead?

The thought roared through on a freight train of fear. But the moment that passed, an odd sort of acceptance settled in. If he was dead, he was dead. There wouldn't be a whole lot of point in getting upset by it.

On the other hand, he didn't feel dead. Not that he knew what it felt like but whatever it was, this wasn't it. He was just...apart...not completely gone. He couldn't move, couldn't even open his eyes, but he could sense certain things. There was something down his throat. The moment he realized it, he thought he was choking. If he'd had the strength, he would have struggled. But he had no strength at all, absolutely none. He was completely helpless.

The realization of that filled him with horror. Death would be better. Could he be paralyzed? Had the crash—he remembered the crash now—done that to him? His heart raced, the only part of him that seemed capable of any action.

Wait, was there something else? He could feel something in his right hand, something warm and soft. Somebody was there. He wasn't alone...

He heard it then, Brenna's voice, speaking very softly, reaching out to him, guiding him back. With a vast surge of relief, he followed.

One month earlier...

Shane signed the chit for the room service waiter, thanked him and shut the door. The room was in darkness, the curtains drawn against the night. Finding his way carefully, he set the tray down on the table beside the bed, then slipped back under the covers.

Brenna lay on her side, her legs slightly drawn up. He drew her close, nestling her against him. She murmured drowsily.

"I've got something for you," Shane said.

"Hmmm..."

"Something you'll really like."

She opened one eye. "I just had something I really like."

He laughed. "Something else."

She made a little, uninterested noise and snuggled back down into the bed.

"Hot cocoa."

Both her eyes opened. "Really?"

"With marshmallows." He turned her over so that she was beneath him. She felt warm, soft, yielding, all woman. "Or whipped cream...or cinnamon sticks...all the trimmings."

"Oooh." She pushed hard against his shoulders, slipped out from under him and stood. He sighed, flopped on his back, and watched her. Naked, she strode over to the tray, surveyed it and smiled. Dipping a finger in the whipped cream, she took her time licking it off.

"You have good ideas," she said when she was done. "Shall I pour?"

She did and very properly. Propped up against the pillows, he accepted his cup but declined to add to it.

"Just one little marshmallow?" she coaxed, holding out the bowl to him. She bent forward slightly at the waist so that her breasts swayed.

"Maybe one..." He took it absently and dropped it into his cup. She returned to the bed with her own, sipped and gave a small sigh of satisfaction. "I still like the beach idea but getting away this weekend has been wonderful."

"We should do it more often." We. He liked the

sound of that. More and more, he was thinking in terms of "we."

She gave him a long, steady look. He had the idea there was a lot more going on in her mind than he could tell. "Yes," she said. "We should."

"Want to go downstairs for dinner?" he asked after a bit.

"Did I ever tell you about the secret thrill I get from room service?"

"Really, secret thrill?"

"Sure. You get to pick out all the things you'd never fix for yourself or even necessarily order in public and someone brings them to you. You can eat in bed and wear anything you want, or nothing at all. When you're done, there are no dishes. It's better than home, it's better than a restaurant, it's…" On a luxurious sigh, she concluded, "…room service."

"To think, all these years on the road, I just thought of it as a way to fend off starvation."

"What you missed."

"Well, no more." He reached across her and plucked the leather-bound menu off the table. "Let's see what we've got here."

Thirty minutes later, when dinner arrived, Brenna hid in the bathroom. She wasn't dressed for company.

"You can come out now," Shane called when they were alone again. "It's just us and the chateaubriand."

She emerged wearing a smile and a white silk nightgown that would have done a 1920s movie star proud. Unadorned, the fabric was smoothed over her body to show every line and curve, the swelling of her nipples, the indentation of her naval, the shadowed cleft between her legs.

"Like it?" she asked, posing by the door.

He shrugged off the toweling robe he'd briefly donned. "What do you think?"

"I think it's a shame dinner would get cold."

"Some priorities you've got."

"Woman does not live by cocoa alone, or anything else for that matter."

He pulled a chair out for her. She smiled her thanks. They sat. Music played in the background. Candles were lit. He poured the wine. They touched glasses.

"Now do you see why I like room service?"

"You have a point," he conceded. "We couldn't sit in a restaurant looking like this."

"You especially couldn't. There'd be a riot."

"Flatterer. So tell me about your first time."

Her eyebrows rose. "Excuse me?"

"For room service."

"Oh, that. All right…it was in Boston. I had just turned twenty-two and I was attending my first conference. After a long day of meetings, workshops and so on, I was dog tired. A bunch of people I knew were going out but I begged off and came back to my room. You see—" She leaned forward confidingly. "I noticed the menu when I unpacked. It was right out there on the table for anyone to see. I even—" her voice dropped a notch "…looked through it."

He nodded solemnly. "So, you already had something in mind?"

"It's true, I did. I ordered a hamburger, medium

rare, with French fries, onion rings and a salad. It was there in twenty-two minutes. All I had to do was sign for it.''

She savored the memory. "I ate on the bed. There was a Mel Gibson movie on pay-for-view. It was heaven.''

"So that was the beginning?"

"That was it. I've never looked back."

He refilled her wineglass. "What was the best room service you ever had?''

She thought for a moment. A slow smile lifted the corners of her mouth. "You know, I've got a funny feeling this is going to be it.''

"Better than Mel on pay-for-view?"

Her eyes ran over his bare chest. "Hmmm, better than that.''

After dinner they danced, very close and very slow. Brenna was all warm silk, slender curves and pure femininity. The bed beckoned. But before he could move toward it, Shane's arm brushed the drapes, parting them just enough to catch a glimpse outside. What he saw stopped him.

"Look," he said and drew her to the window.

The sky was afire. Vast, sweeping arcs of light soared across the heavens. Luminous bands of blue, green and gold dissolved the darkness. They appeared to dance to silent music, as though in obedience to an invisible hand.

"I never get used to seeing the northern lights," Brenna said softly. "They're a glory that can't be remembered. Each time is the first.''

Standing there at the window, holding her in his

arms, Shane agreed. They stared out into the night, watching without words. None were needed. Down below, they could see others, coming outside despite the cold, drawn by a spectacle unequaled even in the most vivid imagination.

He wondered for a fleeting moment if the little girl, Melanie, was still awake. Was she seeing this, too? He hoped she was and that she would remember it more than the fear she had felt at being lost.

"How would you explain this to someone who had never seen it before?" Brenna asked.

He thought for a moment. "I'd say it was the video for eternity."

She leaned her head back against his shoulder. "I like that. It seems as though if you could reach out and catch just the tiniest bit of it, it would draw you right up into forever."

The bands of radiant light did look like streams of pure energy, streaking across the skies. He hadn't noticed that before—how much they looked like currents that could draw him right along.

Draw him out of darkness into light...to warmth and touch...to the whisper of sound taking form as a woman's voice...soft, entreating...

Drawing him....

Chapter 24

Sunday

"Mr. Dutton, can you hear me? Mr. Dutton?"

Slowly, Shane opened his eyes. The light was blinding. He closed them for an instant, then tried again. At first, he saw only a blurred mist. Gradually, it resolved into the face of a man.

"My name is Dr. Mathieson, Mr. Dutton. You're in Anchorage, in the hospital. You were brought in by air rescue. You're on a ventilator right now but we're going to try taking you off that. You're in critical condition, Mr. Dutton, but it's a very good sign that you've regained consciousness. Okay now, just relax and we'll have this out—"

Shane took a deep, shuddering breath. His throat felt raw and his chest still hurt, but none of that mattered compared to the sheer relief of being able to breathe on his own.

"Looking good," the doctor said. He glanced at the monitors. "Your blood pressure is stabilizing. We were worried about that because you'd developed septicemia. Do you know what that is?"

"Infection—" He could barely croak but he got the word out.

Mathieson nodded. "From the leg fracture. We've set that, by the way, and with the infection receding, it should heal nicely. You also have pneumonia in both lungs and a concussion. I'd like to get some idea of the extent of that last part so I'm going to ask you a few questions. If this gets to be too much, just tell me."

For the next five minutes or so, they ran through a dozen or so questions. They were basic things—his name, address, occupation, what was the last thing he remembered, who was president. Mathieson kept asking the same questions over but mixing up the order.

Finally, Shane managed to rasp, "If there are any holes in my head, they must not be anywhere vital."

Mathieson laughed. "I'd say you're doing very well," he agreed. "Frankly, we weren't too sure when they brought you in. Your family is on the way but they've been held up by the weather."

"Brenna…"

"She's outside. When she realized you were coming to, she came and got us." He indicated the nurse with him. They both smiled. Shane got the impression they were feeling more relieved than they wanted to let on, and more surprised.

So he'd come that close. It was something to think about—when he had the energy. Right now, he still felt a vaguely strange sensation, as though not being quite rooted in his body. But it was fading fast, almost like a dream. Reality welcomed him back.

"Could you—" Talking was getting harder, not easier.

"I'll get her," the nurse offered.

She returned a moment later with Brenna. He stared hungrily. It was so damn good to see her again. For awhile, he'd thought that wouldn't happen.

"Hi," he murmured.

She came forward slowly. Her face was very drawn. He could feel the tension in her.

"Hi," she said softly.

She looked exhausted. He realized that with a start. Of course, she did. How else would she look? She was a kind and caring woman involved with a man who had just come real close to getting himself killed.

The one thing she most feared and was least able to deal with.

Really great.

"You're off the ventilator," she said. Her smile was no less heartfelt for being wobbly.

"Yeah, I'm a real hotshot, I can breathe on my own."

"Hey, that's a plus. They told you about the pneumonia?"

"And the rest of it. Boy, next time I go camping I'm going to bring along a field hospital."

That actually got a laugh, even if it was very small and weak.

"Camping? Is that what you call it?"

"Unplanned camping?"

"That's funny. Some of us were calling it crashing. You know, the thing where the plane went down really fast."

"Unplanned landing?" He tried, heaven knew he tried, but she wasn't buying any of it.

"You shouldn't be talking."

He shouldn't be doing a lot of things—breathing, living, hoping—but he didn't think he ought to mention any of that.

There was movement by the door. He glanced toward it and saw Bob looking like something the cat had dragged in. Carol was next to him. They were both grinning as though he'd gone and done something wonderful.

"Hey," Bob said, "you're back. Good going."

"Thank God," Carol murmured. She turned her attention to Brenna.

"Lost my plane," Shane said. That was really bothering him. He figured Bob would understand.

"Tough, buddy, but actually you did more than just lose it. Frank said it was pretty much just a smear on the ground."

He *had* to say that? Right in front of Brenna? "It was a controlled landing," Shane rasped.

Bob's eyebrows went so far up they intercepted his receding hairline. "Controlled by gravity. That's what you meant, right?"

Shane sighed. So much for male solidarity. "Damn ice."

"You flew straight into what had to be the humdinger of all inversions. Fact is, you're incredibly lucky to be in one piece. I've got to hand it to you, it takes a hell of a pilot to walk away from that."

Actually, he'd crawled but wild horses couldn't have gotten Shane to correct him.

"We'll need to call the insurance—"

"Did it," Bob said.

"Notify the shipper—"

"Done."

"Reroute flights until we can—"

"Rerouted and when you're ready, I've got specs on replacement aircraft. Anything else?"

"Put your name on my door?"

Bob blinked hard. He looked away for a second. "No, thanks. If you still want to do it when you're ready to move on, that would be great. But you've got to be back in the saddle first."

"Won't be long—" Shane said. Broken leg, concussion, pneumonia, septi-whatsit, he ran down the list. "Maybe a week—"

Off on the side, forgotten, Dr. Mathieson made a choking noise.

"Ten days," Shane said, "tops." Then he spoiled it by coughing. Sweet heaven, that hurt. Whatever they were doping him with, and it felt like a sledgehammer, it still wasn't enough to keep him from grimacing.

"Mr. Dutton needs some rest," Dr. Mathieson said. He stepped in, reasserting himself, and began herding them toward the door none too subtly. "He's still critical and while we're far more optimistic about his recovery than we were even a short time ago, there's no point pressing our luck. Besides, you all look as though you could do with some sleep, too. You can come back in the morning.''

"Wait," Shane said. There was so much he still needed to say to Brenna, so much he hoped to hear.

But she was already out the door, looking over her shoulder at him yet going all the same.

"Tomorrow," Dr. Mathieson said firmly.

"You'll call me if—" Brenna began.

"We won't need to call. He's turned the corner. He's going to be fine. Go home."

The glass-paneled door shut behind them. He could still see Brenna talking with the doctor but he could no longer hear what was being said.

She really did look done in. When had she last slept? What day was it anyway? Mathieson was right. He'd see her again tomorrow, they'd talk then.

A slight smile touched his mouth. Tomorrow. He'd never really thought of time as a luxury but from now on he just might. At the very least, it was a gift.

Like life itself. Life making itself known with every breath he took, with every sensation that stirred within him. Life that he wanted to take hold of, hold fast to, cherish in a way he'd never needed to before.

Tomorrow. He'd see Brenna tomorrow. He'd tell her—everything. And then...

"He's asleep," Dr. Mathieson said to the nurse.

Shane just barely heard him, and then he was.

Brenna was finally home. For a split second, standing at the door, she couldn't quite figure out what to do with the key. It went somewhere but— She snapped back just enough to put it in the lock and turn it. Stumbling into the house, she stood for a moment, so completely drained that she wasn't sure she could take another step.

She'd said good-night to Bob and Carol when they dropped her off, with hugs and a few tears. Carol offered to come with her to the hospital in the morning but she said thanks, but no. It was time for them to start getting back to their lives.

Time for her, too, except she wasn't going to think about that right now. Couldn't think about it, actually, not through the fog of exhaustion that gripped her. Within it, she felt oddly keyed up, her mind racing.

Shane was alive.

Shane was alive.

She had to repeat it, turning it over in her mind, looking at it with wonder. He had come so very close—

No, she wouldn't go in that direction. She would stay with what mattered. He was still very sick but he'd turned the corner. He was going to recover.

"He beat the odds," Dr. Mathieson had said. "To tell you the truth, when they brought him in—"

He didn't have to finish. Brenna understood only too well. She forced herself away from the wall she'd been leaning against—it was more comfortable than she would have guessed—and looked at the stairs to the second floor. Funny how she'd never noticed they were so high.

Her legs felt as though they weighed a hundred pounds each. Slowly, she half climbed, half hauled herself up the stairs and down the hall to her bedroom.

She remembered her bedroom. She'd been in it a million years ago.

She wasn't going to sleep in her clothes. That just wasn't going to happen. But for the first time she could remember, she was going to leave them where they dropped.

Crawling in between the sheets, she groaned. How could just lying down feel so incredibly good? Too bad her brain was on overdrive. She was sure she wouldn't be able to close her eyes. If she could just think of something besides Shane, just stop picturing how he looked in that hospital bed and how much worse it all could have been.

If only—

Her head touched the pillow. She slept.

Chapter 25

Monday

The ringing of the phone woke Brenna. She staggered up through layers of sleep, driven by the keen edge of panic. Dr. Mathieson had said they wouldn't need to call. He said Shane would be fine.

Oh, God, please, no—

"Hello?"

"Hi, Dr. O'Hare? It's Trudi, listen I'm really sorry to bother you but when you didn't come in, I wasn't sure— Uh, I woke you didn't I? Look, never mind, I'll just—"

"Trudi...?" Trudi Blakely, the perky research assistant who looked barely old enough to be let out by herself. That Trudi.

"What time is it?" Brenna asked, even as she fumbled for the clock, knocking it off the table.

"Almost noon. Are you all right? I mean, if this isn't a good time—"

"Noon! How could it be—?"

"Well, you know, it's Monday...the weekend..."

"I won't be coming in today," Brenna said. Still clutching the phone, she stumbled out of bed. She'd never slept until noon in her life. She had to get to the hospital, see Shane—

"Uh, okay, I'll tell everyone. I guess somebody can cover your classes...."

"A friend of mine was in a plane crash. He's in the hospital. I'm on my way back there now."

"Oh, my God, how terrible. That wasn't... Hey, on the news last night, they said that the guy who pulled the men off the tanker, that he'd crashed. That wasn't your friend, was it?"

"That's him but he's going to be fine." Fine, fine, fine, Shane was going to be fine. "I have to go now, Trudi. Bye."

Brenna hung up, yanked clothes from the closet and dashed into the bathroom. Five minutes later, hair still sopping wet, she bolted down the stairs and into her car. The day was clear which was good, but as a result, lunch time traffic was heavier than usual. It seemed like absolutely everyone felt the need to be out and about.

"Damn," Brenna muttered as she pounded her hand against the steering wheel in frustration. How could she have slept so late? Being totally drained physically and emotionally had something to do with it, but even so—

Traffic started moving again. She breathed a sigh

of relief but that didn't last long. It stopped again just a few blocks farther on. By the time she finally pulled into the parking lot next to the hospital, it was almost one o'clock.

She hurried inside and made her way to intensive care. Several people were waiting by the doors to the unit. She glanced at them in passing—two men in their late twenties or early thirties, a woman about the same age and another woman who looked slightly younger.

She was through the doors before she realized that the men looked somewhat familiar. Even as she tried to place them, she was drawn up short. There were people with Shane. An older woman stood near the bed. Beside her was an older man and next to him was a man of about thirty who resembled the two outside.

Of course...the weather had cleared...his family was here.

The older woman glanced up. She saw Brenna. For just a moment she looked uncertain, then she smiled. She said a quick word to the others and came out to meet her.

"You must be Miss O'Hare," the woman said. "I'm Abby Dutton, Shane's mother."

Yes, she was. There was really no mistaking her. Shane had her eyes and the same warm smile. But he got his height and strength from the man who could only be his father. Following his wife, Patrick Dutton introduced himself and held out his hand.

"Nice to meet you, Miss O'Hare. We appreciate your being here for our son when we couldn't be."

"I was glad to do it," Brenna murmured. She felt suddenly self-conscious. How much had Shane said to his parents? Had they even known she existed before today? What impression did they have of their relationship?

For that matter, what was their relationship now? After the fight they'd had, she couldn't presume anything.

"Dr. Mathieson says he believes Shane will come off the critical list tomorrow," Abby Dutton said. For just a moment, she blinked back tears.

"That's wonderful news," Brenna said. "How is his leg doing?"

Patrick Dutton gestured toward the cubicle. "You can ask him yourself. His throat's still sore from the ventilator they had him on but he can talk."

"I really don't want to intrude—"

"Nonsense." Abby took her arm gently. "I know Shane wants to see you."

Mindful that visitors in intensive care were limited—and that more of his family was waiting outside—Brenna hesitated. But the need to have even a moment with Shane proved overwhelming.

She stepped into the cubicle. The younger man shot her a quick look, smiled and said, "Hi, I'm Mike Dutton, Shane's brother."

"Little brother," Shane added. He looked very pale and weary, but he, too, was smiling.

She stepped closer to the bed and took the hand he held out to her. His fingers curled around hers, so much stronger and warmer than only a few hours before.

"You're really better," Brenna said. She was just now letting herself believe it.

"How about that?" He glanced at the others.

"I'd just love a cup of tea," his mother said.

"Maybe something to eat," his father added.

"I'm starved," Mike agreed, "and I'll bet the others are, too."

As one, they headed for the door.

"Oh, no," Brenna said quickly, "there's no need for you to leave." She felt terrible. His family had come so many miles under such desperate circumstances, the last thing she wanted was for them to feel as though they shouldn't be there.

Too late; they were gone. Mr. and Mrs. Dutton had their heads together and were whispering about something or other, Mike just grinned broadly.

Shane sighed. "My family."

"They're very nice."

"They think I'm still twelve." He winced. "God, that sounds awful. It isn't even true. They're just not used to seeing me like this."

"Well, good, I'd hate to think they could be used to it."

"There's a point. So, how're you doing?"

She was sitting on the edge of the bed, unsure of exactly when that had happened. "I'm...fine. Actually, I meant to get here earlier but I overslept."

"You were exhausted." The skin was drawn tautly over his cheekbones. He had lost weight in the last few days and it showed. But apart from that, he looked remarkably well for a man who had come so close to death.

"Dieter and Carl were here. They told me about you being at the airport and all." He cleared his throat. "I'm really sorry you went through this."

"I went through…what about you? You almost—" Her voice broke. Without warning, with absolutely no idea that she was about to do so, she began to cry.

Horrified, she turned away and tried to get up but his hand holding hers stopped her.

"I'm sorry," she murmured, horrified by her loss of control. Her emotions were perilously close to the surface. "I didn't think this would happen…."

Shane drew her closer. She resisted but his strength was returning with remarkable speed. Somehow, she was lying on the bed beside him. His arms were around her and her head was on his chest.

"It's all right," he murmured. "I'm so sorry I put you through this…so sorry. You deserve so much better."

"I do?" Brenna raised her head. She was genuinely puzzled. Why all the emphasis on her when he was the one who had almost died? "What about you? I was so angry, I sent you away and all because you were helping people. I never thought of them or even about you. All I thought of was myself." The anger she felt at herself was unmistakable.

"You had a reason for that," Shane insisted. "What you'd been through as a child. I knew about it and I didn't take it into account the way I should have. Lying out there, realizing that I really could die, made me see things differently."

"How differently?" A tiny shimmer of hope whispered through her. She grabbed hold and let it carry her along.

"I love you, Brenna," he said quietly. I want us to have a future together. If that means giving up rescue work, then that's what it means. I don't want to lose you over that. Hell, I don't want to lose you at all."

His hand cupped the back of her head. His mouth touched hers lightly, tentatively, in a caress that was as cherishing as it was passionate. Brenna shut her eyes against the intensity of emotion that washed over her. It was all within her grasp. Everything she could have hoped for. All she had to do was tell Shane that he was right. He'd be safe, they'd be together. What more could she possibly want?

"You said I was asking you to give up yourself," she murmured.

He stiffened slightly. "That was before. I didn't really understand."

"But you do now?"

"Yes, I do." He looked down at her, his gaze questioning. "What's the matter? I thought you'd be happy."

She smiled ruefully. "I should be but there's a problem." Her fingers touched the curve of his jaw tenderly. He needed to shave. There were dark shadows still under his eyes. With all her being, she wanted him to be safe. It took every ounce of courage she possessed to say what she had to.

"What if Frank and the other pilots who went after you made the same decision you're making? They have families, don't they? People who love them and who I'm sure aren't too happy when they risk their lives. But if they hadn't, you wouldn't be here. How can I say that you shouldn't do what you do, but it's okay for other people to take those chances? I'd be the world's worst hypocrite."

"Honey…do you realize what you're saying?"

"Besides, you're overlooking something or at least you're trying to get me to overlook it."

His gaze narrowed. "What's that?"

"You didn't almost die on a rescue mission. You almost died on a perfectly routine flight. So, what do I do? Ask you to give up flying, your business, your whole life? Sit safe in a corner somewhere? How long would it be before you hated me?"

"I could never hate you…"

"But you wouldn't be happy and you really would lose yourself." Brenna took a deep breath. Far down inside her, a hard core of fear and sorrow began to unravel, giving up the fierce grip it had kept on her for so very long.

"You've been my lover and my friend. But the man who is all of that is the same man who won't let people drown on a sinking tanker while there's a chance he can help them. You can't give up such an important part of yourself and still be the same person."

"And I can't ask you to live with the fear that what happened to your father will happen to me."

She sat up. It was very quiet in the little room. She thought of how that quiet had felt the night before, when she faced the possibility that he would die in the next few hours, that she would never have a chance to tell him how she felt. Now she did have a chance...for that and more...if only she could bring herself to seize it.

"I was a child then and I'm not anymore. I'm a grown woman. A woman who loves you with all her heart. You don't have to ask me to face my fears. That's not your responsibility. It's mine."

A long sigh escaped him. He laid back against the pillow and looked at her for what seemed like a long time. Slowly, he smiled.

"Okay, but there is something else I'd like to ask you."

And he did.

Chapter 26

Six weeks later

"Stop squirming," Carol snapped. "I've almost got this thing fastened...there!" She stepped back and stared at Brenna in the mirror. With complete sincerity, she said, "You look absolutely gorgeous."

Brenna studied the reflection. She saw a pale, slender woman in an off-the-shoulder, ankle-length white silk gown trimmed with embroidered white roses. Her eyes were very large.

"You think so? There's not a deer-in-the-headlights thing going on here?"

"Well, yeah," Carol conceded with a grin. "Maybe a little although why you should be scared is beyond me. Just because you're taking the biggest and most dramatic step of your life..."

"Remind me why we're friends?"

"Because I introduced you to Mr. Perfect?"

Brenna sighed. She picked up the circlet of white roses that held her veil. "You're going to hold that over me forever, aren't you?"

Carol nodded happily. "You bet. However, I may be out of the matchmaking business. Anything after this would just be a letdown."

"Quit while you're ahead?"

"Exactly."

"I still can't believe I'm having this big a wedding..."

All Shane's family was there, of course. Her mom had come up along with assorted aunts, uncles, cousins, nieces and nephews. The Virginia Duttons and the Brooklyn O'Hares had taken to each other at once. Abby Dutton and Marie O'Hare were already such good friends that they might have known each other for years.

Everyone from Air Aleut was on hand as was the entire staff of the lab. Trudi had sworn she was going to bring in a vial of the zoo plankton just so they wouldn't miss the fun. Frank, Dieter, Carl and the rest of the rescue team were there as well.

"Just one thing," Carol said. "Toss the bouquet to Trudi. There's this new guy in the lab, you know, the skinny one with the shoulder-length brown hair. Surely, you've noticed her making cow eyes all over him?"

Actually, Brenna hadn't been noticing much of anything the last few weeks. With Shane in the hospital and then at her place recuperating, it was all she could do to see to the care and watering of the plankton. However, somewhere along the line she'd started liking the new research assistant. Maybe it had to do with being generally delighted with the whole world.

"I think I may be losing my mind," Brenna said.

"And on that romantic note—" Carol opened the door. Organ music swelled. Brenna took a deep breath, realized it wasn't going to do any good and stepped forward.

"I was not," Shane said some time later.

They were in the bedroom of a stone cottage nestled on the hillside above one of the Caribbean's nicer bays. They'd flown down directly from the reception. For a great pilot, Shane made a lousy passenger.

"You were," Brenna insisted. "I saw you. Right when the thingie started making that funny noise, you were gripping your tray as though you could fly the plane with it."

He winced and looked heavenward, or at least at the ceiling where a fan turned lazily. "It's not a *thingie*, it's a thruster, and the noise was perfectly normal."

Brenna threw open the shutters, gazed out at a view that was nothing less than stupendous, and grinned. "Your knuckles were white."

"It was a little rough on the turn, that's all. Some pilots do it that way. I don't. Of course, the guy doesn't really have landings down, either. We bounced—twice."

"Was there anything you liked about the flight?"

"You were on it."

"Stock answer but still worth points. Come on

now, take a look. Isn't this the most beautiful place you've ever seen?''

The sun was just beginning to set. A balmy tropical breeze rustled the palm trees fringing their private beach. Shane's arms went around her. They stood together, wordlessly, looking out until the first stars could be seen.

''They'll be serving dinner soon,'' Shane said. His lips nuzzled her neck right at the precise spot that never failed to—

''Hmmm, but then there's always—''

His voice was low and husky, seductively caressing. ''—room service.''

She shivered delicately. The dress she'd worn for traveling was a lightweight linen sheath belted at the waist. His hands roamed over it at will.

''Hungry?'' he murmured.

''Starved.'' She turned in his arms, moving against him, delighting in his strength. The cast had come off his leg just in time for the wedding. Although they had found certain inventive ways around it, having that impediment gone seemed to put the crash truly behind them.

''Want me to find the menu?'' he asked as he unfastened her belt.

''Eventually.'' The dress had large buttons down the back. He undid them with elaborate patience.

''You picked this dress on purpose, didn't you?''

She opened her eyes wide. ''Me? Do a thing like that?''

''There's some culture where the bride comes to her husband in a gown closed by hundreds of intricate knots. He's expected to undo each of them or be accused of a shameful loss of self-control."

"How far do you think the grooms usually get?"

"As far as the nearest pair of scissors." He undid the last button. The dress fell open. Brenna held her arms out, allowing it to slide off. Her breasts swelled above the lace trimming of a teal silk Victorian corselet cut high on her hips.

"You've outdone yourself," Shane murmured.

She smiled and began unbuttoning his shirt. "It's the something blue."

"Right...blue..." He seemed very distracted. His shirt joined her dress on the floor. Brenna ran her hands over his chest. During his recuperation, he'd insisted on working out every day, pushing himself to the absolute limit. If anything, he was in even more magnificent shape than before.

She eased out of her shoes as she slowly undid his zipper. Beneath her hand, he was warm and hard. Tracing the curve of his ear with her tongue, she whispered, "You know, they have room service here twenty-four hours a day, whenever we happen to get around to it."

Shane lifted her. With three quick strides, he was at the side of the bed. He laid Brenna down, pausing just long enough to strip off the rest of his clothes before joining her. Framing her face with his hands, he smiled down into the joyful blue eyes of his wife.

"That's perfect," he said.

"Isn't it?" she answered and opened her arms to him.

* * * * *

COMING NEXT MONTH

#781 NIGHTHAWK—Rachel Lee
Conard County
After being wrongly accused of a crime he hadn't committed,
Craig Nighthawk just wanted to be left alone. Then he met
Esther Jackson, who was fighting her own battles but needed his
protection to make peace with her past…and ensure a future for them
both.

#782 IN MEMORY'S SHADOW—Linda Randall Wisdom
Single mom Keely Harper had returned to Echo Ridge to build a new
life. But when terrifying memories came flooding back, she sought
safety in the arms of town sheriff Sam Barkley. He knew the truth about
her past, and he was willing to go above and beyond the call of duty to
safeguard this troubled mother.

#783 EVERY WAKING MOMENT—Doreen Roberts
U.S. Marshal Blake Foster should have known better than to get
involved with prime murder suspect Gail Stevens. But now was too late
for regrets. Time was running out to prove her innocence—and his own
love—because Gail had fallen into the hands of the real killer….

#784 AND DADDY MAKES THREE—Kay David
Becoming a dad to the daughter he'd never known about meant that
Grayston Powers had to marry her guardian, Annie Burns, because
Annie wasn't about to abandon the child she considered her own. They
insisted it was a marriage in name only…but could they really deny the
passion between them?

#785 McCAIN'S MEMORIES—Maggie Simpson
Defense attorney Lauren Hamilton had a weakness for sexy bad boys,
and Jon McCain, her rugged amnesiac client, certainly fit the bill. She
needed him to remember something, *anything*, to help her clear his
name. Because her case—and her heart—hinged on the secrets of this
man without a memory….

#786 GABRIEL IS NO ANGEL—Wendy Haley
Rae Ann Boudreau would do *any*thing to serve a summons on a
deadbeat dad—even if it meant going undercover as a belly dancer.
Vice cop Gabriel MacLaren would do *any*thing to protect his star
snitch—but falling for the gorgeous process server who was threatening
his case hadn't been part of the plan….

Take 4 bestselling love stories FREE

Plus get a FREE surprise gift!

Special Limited-time Offer

Mail to Silhouette Reader Service™

3010 Walden Avenue
P.O. Box 1867
Buffalo, N.Y. 14240-1867

YES! Please send me 4 free Silhouette Intimate Moments® novels and my free surprise gift. Then send me 6 brand-new novels every month, which I will receive months before they appear in bookstores. Bill me at the low price of $3.34 each plus 25¢ delivery and applicable sales tax, if any.* That's the complete price and a savings of over 10% off the cover prices—quite a bargain! I understand that accepting the books and gift places me under no obligation ever to buy any books. I can always return a shipment and cancel at any time. Even if I never buy another book from Silhouette, the 4 free books and the surprise gift are mine to keep forever.

245 BPA A3UW

Name	(PLEASE PRINT)	
Address	Apt. No.	
City	State	Zip

This offer is limited to one order per household and not valid to present Silhouette Intimate Moments® subscribers. *Terms and prices are subject to change without notice. Sales tax applicable in N.Y.

UMOM-696   ©1990 Harlequin Enterprises Limited

As seen on TV!
Free Gift Offer

With a Free Gift proof-of-purchase from any Silhouette® book,
you can receive a beautiful cubic zirconia pendant.

This gorgeous marquise-shaped stone is a genuine cubic
zirconia—accented by an 18" gold tone necklace.
(Approximate retail value $19.95)

Send for yours today...
compliments of ▼ *Silhouette*®

To receive your free gift, a cubic zirconia pendant, send us one original proof-of-
purchase, photocopies not accepted, from the back of any Silhouette Romance™,
Silhouette Desire®, Silhouette Special Edition®, Silhouette Intimate Moments®
or Silhouette Yours Truly™ title available in February, March and April at your favorite
retail outlet, together with the Free Gift Certificate, plus a check or money order for
$1.65 U.S./$2.15 CAN. (do not send cash) to cover postage and handling, payable
to Silhouette Free Gift Offer. We will send you the specified gift. Allow 6 to 8 weeks for
delivery. Offer good until April 30, 1997 or while quantities last. Offer valid in the
U.S. and Canada only.

Free Gift Certificate

Name: _____

Address: _____

City: _____ State/Province: _____ Zip/Postal Code: _____

Mail this certificate, one proof-of-purchase and a check or money order for postage
and handling to: SILHOUETTE FREE GIFT OFFER 1997. In the U.S.: 3010 Walden
Avenue, P.O. Box 9077, Buffalo NY 14269-9077. In Canada: P.O. Box 613, Fort Erie,
Ontario L2Z 5X3.

FREE GIFT OFFER   084-KFD
ONE PROOF-OF-PURCHASE
To collect your fabulous FREE GIFT, a cubic zirconia pendant, you must include this
original proof-of-purchase for each gift with the properly completed Free Gift Certificate.

084-KFD

At last the wait is over...
In March
New York Times bestselling author

NORA ROBERTS

will bring us the latest from the Stanislaskis as
Natasha's now very grown-up stepdaughter,
Freddie, and Rachel's very sexy brother-in-law
Nick discover that love is worth waiting for in

WAITING FOR NICK

Silhouette Special Edition #1088

and in April
visit Natasha and Rachel again—or meet them
for the first time—in

The Stanislaski Sisters

**containing TAMING NATASHA
and FALLING FOR RACHEL**

Available wherever Silhouette books are sold.

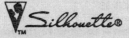